M000234731

Other Series by Harper Lin

The Patisserie Mysteries

The Emma Wild Holiday Mysteries

The Wonder Cats Mysteries

www.HarperLin.com

Margaritas, Marzipan, and Murder

A Cape Bay Café Mystery Book 3

Harper Lin

ISBN-13: 978-1987859270
ISBN-10: 1987859278

Contents

Chapter 1   7
Chapter 2   21
Chapter 3   35
Chapter 4   49
Chapter 5   63
Chapter 6   78
Chapter 7   93
Chapter 8   111
Chapter 9   122
Chapter 10   136
Chapter 11   150
Chapter 12   165
Chapter 13   176
Chapter 14   190
Chapter 15   204
Chapter 16   218
Chapter 17   230
Chapter 18   245
Chapter 19   257
Chapter 20   269

Recipe 1: Marzipan   281
Recipe 2: Classic Margarita on the Rocks   283
Recipe 3: Frozen Strawberry Margarita   284

About the Author   285

Chapter One

"To Sammy!" Dawn said, lifting her margarita glass in the air for a toast.

"To Sammy," I echoed, clinking my glass against Dawn's and Sammy's. "To her freedom!"

"Hear, hear," Dawn cheered as Sammy blushed.

The three of us—me, Sammy, and Dawn, Sammy's best friend since preschool—were gathered on the oceanfront deck of Fiesta Mexicana, Cape Bay's best and only Mexican restaurant, to celebrate Sammy's breakup with her longtime loser boyfriend, Jared.

They'd been together for ten years, since their senior year in high school, and Jared had been refusing to move their relationship beyond boyfriend-girlfriend status for almost as long, always claiming that it would break his mother's heart if he left her to get married.

Even so, Sammy had held out hope for a ring for their one-year anniversary, then their five-year, then their ten-year anniversary a few weeks ago. In the last case, the big surprise he'd promised her turned out to be an evening of go-karting. When that happened, even I, who hadn't known her well for all that long, asked her what she was still doing with him. She said it was because she loved him. I let it go. But Dawn didn't.

"God, I'm glad I finally convinced you to break up with him," Dawn said, coming up from a long drink from her glass. We had been at the bar less than half an hour, but she had ordered a second round, despite Sammy and me having made nowhere near the impact on our drinks that she had. I'd never gone out with Dawn before, but I could already tell she was either going to be a lot of fun or no fun at all. She was that kind of girl.

"Fran did some convincing, too," Sammy said, nodding in my direction.

I looked at her with my eyebrows raised as I swallowed the sip I'd just taken. The margarita was made just the way I liked it: a little tart, a little sweet, a little salty, and exactly the right amount of burn from the tequila. "I did?" I asked after the liquid had made its way down my throat.

"You did."

"What did I say?" I asked.

"It wasn't so much what you said as the fact that you said it. It was one thing when Dawn told me I needed to break up with him. I mean, she's been saying that for years."

"Nine and a half years to be exact," Dawn interjected. "Maybe nine and three quarters."

Sammy rolled her eyes with a smile and a shake of her head at her best friend. Clearly, they'd had the same conversation more than once. "Anyway, I've been hearing about it from Dawn for years, but when you said something after we've only really known each other for a few months…"

I looked down at my glass, embarrassed that I'd been so blunt. It was very un-New-England-y of me. Well, being blunt was very New England, but sticking my nose in someone else's business wasn't. Who someone else chose to spend their time with was none of my concern, even if I did think they were making a huge mistake. "I'm sorry," I said. "I shouldn't have pried into your personal life."

"Don't be sorry," Sammy exclaimed.

"Please," Dawn chimed in. "If that's what it took to get the girl to see reason, I'm glad you said something!" She tipped her glass up and emptied it.

"Still—" I started.

"Still nothing," Sammy said, looking me dead in the eye. "I'd been with him for ten *years*, Fran, always telling myself it didn't matter that he didn't want to get married, that it was fine if he never wanted to go away for a weekend because his mom would be all alone, that birthdays and anniversaries weren't really that big of a deal so it was okay if he never wanted to do anything special to celebrate. Ten years! Do you know how many of my friends I've watched get married and have kids in that time?" Sammy's face was getting flushed as she ranted.

"Do you know how many times I've been asked when we were getting engaged?" she went on. "And I couldn't even be one of those people who just says they're not the marrying kind or something, because I *am* the marrying kind. It's all I've wanted for ten years! Jared just kept saying he wasn't ready." She waved her margarita glass in the air.

She was so worked up that she didn't even notice that some of it sloshed over the side and fell onto the deck floor. I reached out, took it from her hand, and placed it on the table. She kept going without missing a beat.

"I had to keep telling people we were waiting until we were a little older, a little more established, had a little more money. It was so embarrassing! And then when I had to tell you that my big anniversary date was go-karts? Ugh! I wanted to sink into the floor and disappear! And what was my excuse? That I loved him? When that's how he treated me?" She stopped and shook her head. "I'm just glad I finally realized it before I wasted any more time on him."

I was surprised and impressed by Sammy's outburst. It was so far out of character for her. Sammy's usual disposition was as sunny as her blond hair. She smiled a lot, laughed a lot, got along with everybody, and made customers at the café smile. She rarely got worked up about anything, and on the incredibly rare occasion that she did, she never had that much to say about it. I liked seeing that kind of spunk and passion from her.

Not knowing what else to say, I raised my glass toward Sammy. "To getting out and not wasting time on losers!"

"I'll drink to that!" Dawn said, clinking her glass against mine and Sammy's.

The waiter had brought the second round while Sammy was venting about Jared. Dawn tipped it back and drank so much I felt reasonably confident we'd be on to the third round soon. Of course, if we kept going at our current pace, she could just drink Sammy's or mine. She'd be ready for her next one long before we were.

"You know, I gotta say, Sam, I am glad you're finally done feeling sorry for yourself about the breakup. Jared was a loser and not worth all the crying you were doing over him, was he, Fran?" Dawn said.

The native New Englander in me wanted to make a noncommittal grunt, but apparently my opinion had meant something to Sammy before.

"I can't fault you for crying. I know I cried my share of tears when I found out my fiancé was cheating on me. But it's definitely good to see you getting past the really depressed phase. He didn't deserve you, and you deserve to be happy."

Sammy gave me a small, grateful smile. I knew from my own recent experience that Dawn's tough-love attitude was sometimes exactly what the doctor ordered, but other times, you needed someone to tell you that whatever you were feeling was fine and that they were there for you no matter how long it took you to get back to normal. Between the two of us, we had Sammy's emotional needs covered. But that, I suspected, was why I'd been invited along.

The night out on the town had been Dawn's idea. She'd come into the café the evening before, after Sammy had gone home but before I closed up shop. I didn't know Dawn personally, but she came into the café sometimes after Sammy's shifts to hang out with her.

She burst through the door unceremoniously, calling out before she even had the chance to see that I was standing right at the counter.

"Fran!" she bellowed. "We have to do something about Sammy!"

"We do?" I asked.

"For God's sake, yes!" she said, slamming her hands down on the counter. "She's been moping around, crying her eyes out for a week now. I can't take it anymore!"

You can't take it anymore? Sammy's the one with the broken heart. But at the same time, I understood where she was coming from. Sammy had been doing okay at work—not breaking down in tears or anything like that, at least not after the first day or two—but she definitely wasn't her normal, cheery, ebullient self.

"What do you want me to do?" I asked Dawn.

While I considered Sammy a friend, she was also my employee. I'd known her for a long time but had only really gotten to know her personally over the past couple of months since I'd returned to Cape Bay from New York City. I really wasn't sure I was the right person to help break her out of her funk.

Dawn looked at me as if I was stupid. "We need to take her out. Like, to party. Girls' night out. I know that's not just a Massachusetts thing. I watch TV. They have girls' nights out in New York."

"Even if they didn't, I'm from Massachusetts."

She didn't look as though she believed me.

"Really!" *She knew that, didn't she? That I'd moved back to Cape Bay to take over the café after my mother died? That I grew up here?*

"I know," she replied coolly. "You were just away so long, I thought maybe you forgot."

"Forgot the girls' nights out that we also have in New York?"

She gave me that "are you stupid?" look again then shook her head as if she couldn't be bothered. "We need to take Sammy out," she said, giving up on explaining the concept of "girls' night out" to me.

"Do you really think Sammy would want me there? I mean, I'm her boss."

"And her friend. Of course she would want you there. Are you free tomorrow night?"

Even though I knew it would take Sammy some time to get over the breakup since she'd been with Jared for so long, I couldn't help but think that it would do her some good to get out, have a little fun, and remember that there was a big world out there as soon as she was ready to rejoin it. So I had agreed to Dawn's plan for a girls' night out.

And that was how we'd ended up on the deck of Fiesta Mexicana, tipping back margaritas and breathing in the salty sea air. It was the last week of the summer tourist season, and you could already feel the chill creeping into the air. Labor Day was coming up on Monday, the kids would go back to school on Tuesday, and Cape Bay's tourist traffic would be confined to the weekends for the next six weeks until Columbus Day, when it essentially ground to a halt.

There would be a few tourists over the holidays and Valentine's Day, but it wouldn't be anything noteworthy until the spring breakers invaded in March, after which it would stop again until the season started on Memorial Day weekend. After the emotionally and physically exhausting summer, my mother's sudden death, and the long hours I'd been working at the café, I was more than ready for the slower pace of winter.

Dawn downed the last of her drink and stood up. "I'll be back. Gotta hit the little girls' room."

I watched her walk away then looked over at Sammy, who was staring out at the ocean. The sun had long since set, but the full moon lit the water up brightly enough that the people walking along the beach didn't bother turning their flashlights on to light their way. It was a perfect late-summer night, but I could tell from Sammy's face that she wasn't really enjoying it.

"You okay?" I asked her quietly.

She nodded without taking her eyes off the water. The light from the neon beer sign behind her shone down on her hair, creating a halo effect. It wasn't the first time the word "cherubic" had come to my mind in relation to Sammy, although it was usually the smiling cherubs I thought she looked like, not the tearful ones.

"It'll get better," I said. I knew from experience. It had only been a few months since my then-fiancé had broken the news that he was leaving me for the girl in his office he'd been cheating on me with. The first couple of weeks had been agonizing, and then when I wasn't looking, the cloud began to lift.

She turned away from the water and looked at me, the corner of her mouth twitching up while her eyes stayed sad. "Promise?"

"Promise," I replied. "It might seem like forever, but things will be looking up before you know it."

The door from the deck to the patio opened, and Dawn walked through. She moved slowly, and I thought I detected a wobble in her step as she passed the table next to ours. I nudged Sammy and nodded in Dawn's direction. Sammy's eyes got big, and she started to stand, but before she could get up, Dawn lunged into the chair closest to her.

Dawn's head tipped back, coming so close to the woman sitting at the table next to us that it nearly rested on her shoulder. Sammy and I looked at each other again. I wasn't sure what was wrong with Dawn, and from Sammy's expression, I guessed that she didn't either.

"Dawn, are you—" I started, leaning across the table toward her.

Her head snapped forward, and one finger flew to her lips. "Shhhhh!" Her eyes were round and intense as she looked at me then at Sammy. After a few seconds, she leaned back again and turned her face upward.

I leaned over to Sammy and whispered, "Is she okay?"

Sammy shook her head and shrugged, no surer of Dawn's condition than I was.

I looked back at Dawn, who was still inexplicably staring at the ceiling, her shoulder-length, rust-colored hair actually falling over the back of the other woman's chair. The people at that table had just been seated, and they were chatting as they looked over their menus, too absorbed in what they were doing to notice that Dawn had practically joined their party.

I had no idea what was going on with her. She had seemed fine before she left the table. And she'd seemed okay—strange, but fine—when she'd sat up and shushed us. She'd only had two drinks, and she'd been right there with us until she'd gone to the bathroom.

No one except the waiter had come near us. I didn't think she'd had enough alcohol to be drunk, and unless someone had intercepted her on her way to the bathroom, I couldn't imagine that she'd been drugged. That wasn't even something I would have worried about going out with girlfriends in New York, let alone sleepy little Cape Bay.

Something was very wrong; I just didn't know what.

Chapter Two

I watched Dawn for what seemed like an eternity but was probably only a few seconds. Sammy was still watching Dawn and looking as confused as I was. I tucked my long brown hair behind my ears to try to hear better what Dawn was listening to, but with the chatters of the restaurant patrons around me, I still couldn't make out the words.

Finally, I decided I couldn't just let her sit there all limp and not do anything. I reached out toward Dawn to see if I could get her attention by tapping on the table.

Before I could even tap once, she popped up and leaned her elbows on the table. She stared at me as if I was crazy for having my arm stretched across the table. I pulled it back, knowing it wasn't worth trying to explain that we thought she had passed out.

"Did you hear what they're talking about?" she whispered.

So that was what she had been doing—eavesdropping on the neighboring table. It almost made sense, though it would have been less weird for her to have told Sammy and me what she was doing.

From what I knew of Dawn, eavesdropping was something she would do. She seemed to have a constant expectation that everyone around her should understand what was going on in her head. I certainly didn't. Maybe Sammy did, based on how unfazed she seemed by Dawn's return to the land of the living. But then again, maybe Sammy was just used to Dawn's quirks.

When neither of us admitted to eavesdropping on the conversation next to us—perhaps because we were distracted by Dawn's strange behavior—she filled us in. "They found a body!"

"They did?" I asked, gesturing toward the other table.

"No, not them," Dawn said, looking disgusted. "They," she repeated, making air quotes. "Like, people in general. A body was found."

"Where?" I asked. "Here in Cape Bay?"

She rolled her eyes. I was convinced she thought I was too dense to tie my own shoes. "Yes, here in Cape Bay! Where else?"

"I would prefer anywhere else," Sammy said.

I lifted my margarita glass and tapped it against hers. I could drink to not finding a body in Cape Bay. We'd had enough of those lately—first my boyfriend Matt's father and then a local kickboxing student. It would be fine by me if no one found another dead body in town ever again.

"Where?" I asked. "Where in Cape Bay, I mean?" I clarified before Dawn could lose her eyeballs in the back of her head.

"Right next to Mary Ellen's," Dawn said. Mary Ellen's Souvenirs and Gifts was located on Main Street, just a couple of blocks from my café. "They said the cops are still there. You wanna go check it out?"

"The body?" I asked.

"Yeah! Why not? Have you ever seen a real crime scene before, like not on a cop show?"

"Yes," I replied.

I had the unfortunate distinction of being the one to find my neighbor's body—my now-boyfriend Matt's dad—when he was murdered, and I had been there when they processed the scene. Of course, they hadn't known he had been murdered at first, so it hadn't been like on TV at all, but I still wasn't too keen on seeing another corpse.

"Oh yeah," Dawn said.

I could see the wheels turning in her head as she tried to think of another reason for us to visit the crime scene. I finished my drink as I waited for her to land on another idea.

"Do you think Mary Ellen needs us?" Sammy asked.

I immediately realized I wasn't going to win. If Sammy was on Dawn's side, there was no getting out of it, especially since I thought Sammy had a good point. If somebody had been found dead next to Mary Ellen's shop, she'd probably be pretty freaked out.

In a small town like Cape Bay, we all supported each other, especially the shop-keepers. I knew if a body was found next to my café, Mary Ellen would be right there to help me in any way she could. Still, I couldn't concede my point that easily.

"Sammy and I haven't even started our second drinks, and you already ordered a third round," I pointed out. "We can't let all that money and perfectly good alcohol go to waste."

Dawn didn't miss a beat. She stood and picked up the two untouched glasses from the table. She turned around and placed them on the table she'd been eavesdropping on.

"Here you go, ladies! We've been unexpectedly called away and won't be able to finish our drinking. Here are two delicious, untouched margaritas for you to enjoy. This one is your classic margarita on the rocks, and this pretty pink frozen one here is strawberry."

One of the women looked as if she wanted to speak. Before she could, Dawn spotted the waiter coming with our third round perched on his tray and bellowed, "And just in time, here's the rest of them! Put them right here, Alberto." She gestured for him to place them on the strangers' table. "We have another classic on the rocks, another frozen strawberry, and this one here"—she picked up the drink she'd ordered for herself—"is top-shelf and mango. Who wants it?" She glanced around the table, her gaze landing on the woman closest to the window. "You? You look like a girl who appreciates fine liquor." She set the drink down in front of the woman and immediately reached in her own jeans pocket, pulling out a few bills. She handed them to Alberto. "Keep the change, my friend." She turned back to us. "You ready to go?"

"Guess so," I said, standing up. Dawn had made my one solid objection disappear in the blink of an eye and had managed to convince a group of women that drinks from a stranger's table were suitable for consumption. It was kind of impressive and, I suspected, evidence of how good Dawn was at her bartending job.

Sammy swallowed the last of her drink, grabbed her purse, and stood up. "All right, let's go."

Even though it was Sammy's comment about Mary Ellen that convinced us to head to the crime scene, I couldn't tell whether she was actually happy about going or not.

I had a feeling she wasn't exactly enjoying herself and was just ready to leave.

We headed out of the restaurant and made our way into the heart of town. Fiesta Mexicana was situated at the end of the mile-long boardwalk that ran the length of Cape Bay's beachfront.

Main Street ran perpendicular to the beach at the middle of the boardwalk. Mary Ellen's shop was a couple of blocks up from the beach, and my café was a little beyond that. It wasn't a long walk, especially on such a nice night.

If I'd had my way, I would have gone down and sat on the beach to watch the waves crash under the moon. But between Sammy and Mary Ellen, I knew I was needed elsewhere.

Soon, we could see the flashing red and blue lights of the police cars and an ambulance parked outside Mary Ellen's shop. It looked like the entirety of Cape Bay's police force—all nine of them—was out to aid in the investigation.

To be fair, it was still tourist season, so the police department had an extra handful of officers on staff as seasonal help, but the group was still only a fraction of the size of what would have been assembled in New York City for the discovery of a body. The ambulance wasn't even ours—it was from the county EMS station in the next town over.

From what I could see, the police also had a spotlight shining into the alley next to Mary Ellen's store. The light actually belonged to the town. I remembered seeing it set up during Cape Bay's annual Founders' Day celebration.

A big crowd of people was gathered around the group of police cars blocking the road.

Dawn was shameless and walked right past the police cars up to the crime scene tape, which was strung from the corners of the buildings on either side of the alley and around parking meters at the road. A swarm of blue uniforms blocked our view, but Dawn angled and craned her neck to see between them.

"I can see him!" she hissed back at us.

"And?" I asked, not sure I wanted to know.

"Pretty sure he's dead."

It was my turn to roll my eyes. The phrase "a body" didn't typically refer to a living body.

"Would you idiots stop standing there and try doing some police work?" someone shouted from behind the police tape. The voice was familiar, but between my years in Cape Bay and my work at the café, I knew just about everyone on the police force.

"What do you want us to do, Detective?" one of the officers asked.

The detective sighed heavily. "Oh, for the love of..." Heavy footsteps moved toward us. "You," the detective said. "Get a camera. Take pictures. Get everything from every angle. Use a ruler so we know how big things are. You, go with him. You, call the medical examiner's office and find out when somebody's going to be here. I want this body off my street."

The officers gradually dispersed to their different tasks, revealing the scene in the alley. Just as Dawn had said, there was a body, presumably dead as evidenced by both the fact that the paramedics weren't attending to it and that it was covered by a sheet. I was grateful for that.

There were little yellow tents scattered around, marking bits of evidence that mostly seemed to be rocks and bits of trash you'd expect to find in an alley. I remembered seeing on one of those police procedurals with the hot older man lead detective that the police had to consider all trash important until they could be sure it didn't have any blood or footprints on it. I was glad I didn't have that job.

On one side of the sheet-draped body–a man's body, I guessed, from the size and shape of it–was a plastic bag full of... something I couldn't identify. A chill went up my spine when I saw what was on the other side of the body–a gun.

Sammy must have spotted it at the same time. "Was he shot?" she whispered.

I instinctively reached one hand back toward her. Judging by how tight she gripped it, I knew the sight bothered her as much as it did me.

Dawn, however, seemed mostly unaf-fected. "Yeah, I think so." She got up on her tiptoes and leaned to her right. "I think that's blood over there." She pointed toward the body.

"Okay, that's it, let's go," I said. Still holding Sammy's hand, I turned and pulled her along with me back through the police cars and over to the grassy median a block away, near where the ambulance was parked. Sammy's face looked pale in the yellow-orange streetlight,

"Are you okay?" I asked.

"Yeah, just..." She stopped and shuddered. "Another murder."

"Actually, it looks like a suicide," a man's voice said. The dark-haired police officer had been standing just around the corner of the ambulance out of our view but apparently well within earshot. He stepped toward us. "So nothing for you to worry about," he said with a smile at Sammy and me. As he looked at each of us, his eyes lingered for just a second longer on Sammy. "You all right, miss?"

"Yes, I'm fine."

"Are you sure?" His brow furrowed. "You need to sit down? Here, let me help." He popped open the handle on the back of the ambulance door. "Sit down here."

"I'm fine, really. I—"

"Sit down," he repeated firmly. "Don't want to have another body on the ground."

Sammy and I both looked at him, startled by his comment.

"No, I-I mean... sorry, cop humor. I just meant that you looked like you might pass out. And then you'd be..." He gestured toward the ground then shook his head. "Sorry, bad joke."

Sammy sat down on the back of the ambulance. "It's okay. I make coffee jokes sometimes when I'm stressed at work."

The cop chuckled and ran his fingers across his close-cropped hair. "Yeah? You work at a coffee shop?"

"Just up the street," she said, pointing in the direction of the café. "Antonia's Italian Café. I work with Fran here. She owns the place." She motioned to me.

"Oh yeah?" he replied with a smile. "I haven't been there yet. I'll have to come by sometime and see you."

Sammy looked at him curiously, and I knew she was wondering the same thing I was: how had a Cape Bay police officer not been into Antonia's?

The officer must have read her expression, too, a handy skill for someone who had to suss out criminals for a living. "I'm new," he said. "Just moved here from Buffalo."

"What brings you to town?" I asked.

"Family. I grew up in Plymouth. I've been out in New York for a while and just wanted to get back home."

"Well, welcome to Cape Bay! Come into the café any time. Between me and Sammy, one of us is almost always there. We'll get you a cup of coffee on the house."

"Don't let her fool you," Sammy said before he could reply. "Police and firefighters always get free coffee."

I gave her a dirty look for blowing my secret.

The cop laughed. "Well, thank you... Fran, was it?"

"Francesca Amaro," I said, extending my hand. "And we're happy to do it. It's a long-standing family tradition." Back when my grandparents started the café nearly seventy years ago, they gave free food and coffee to the police and firefighters who protected the town as a way of not just thanking them for what they did but also to establish Antonia's as part of the community.

"I'm Ryan Leary," he said, shaking my hand. His hand was huge and strong, and his handshake was just on this side of uncomfortable. I suspected it was a carefully practiced technique. He gave Sammy a questioning look.

"Samantha Eriksen," she said, reaching her hand up to him from where she was still sitting on the back of the ambulance. "Sammy."

"Sammy," he repeated with a smile. "You look like your color's coming back a little."

I wasn't sure whether it was that or if she was blushing, but she did seem to be getting some pink back in her skin.

"Leary!" someone bellowed.

"Right here, Detective," Ryan called, turning and raising one hand in the air.

Detective Mike Stanton stalked into view, and the second he saw me, I knew I was in trouble.

Chapter Three

Mike's stare probably only lasted a few seconds, but it seemed like almost an eternity before his eyes shifted to Sammy. Ryan stood by uneasily, obviously confused about why his boss had gone from urgently demanding his presence to silently staring at Sammy and me.

"You okay, Sam?" Mike finally asked.

"Yeah," she said, standing up quickly from her seat on the ambulance. She dusted her hands off on her jeans. "Just, uh, just needed to sit down for a minute." She managed to flash him a weak smile.

Mike studied her for another few seconds and then turned to me.

"So you two were just walking by when Sammy—what?—started to feel lightheaded and needed to sit down?"

"Sort of. We're actually here with Dawn. We were having a girls' night out—" I started to explain.

"Dawn?" Mike interrupted. Based on his tone, I was almost surprised he didn't pull his little investigator's notebook out of his breast pocket and start taking notes.

"Dawn..." I tried to pull her last name from the dredges of my memory.

"There you are!" Dawn shouted, bounding over to us. "I've been looking everywhere for you guys. You just took off, and I was standing there talking to myself like a weirdo!"

"Oh, *Dawn*," Mike said, clearly realizing which Dawn I was referring to and, I guessed, putting together how our girls' night out had turned into a girls' night at a crime scene.

"Yes, *Dawn*," she repeated. "How are you doin', Mikey?" She punched his arm affectionately, and I wondered if it was legal to hit a police officer in uniform, even if it was playful. I also wondered when someone had last called him "Mikey." He and I had gone to school together from kindergarten all the way through high school, and I couldn't remember anyone calling him "Mikey" after about second grade.

"I'd rather be home with my wife and kids, but other than that, I'm good, Dawn. How are you?" Mike replied, ignoring both her punch and her nickname for him.

"Good! You know, girls' night out tonight. Celebrating Sammy's breakup!" Dawn bounced as she spoke, and I wouldn't have been surprised if she took off to run a lap or two around the ambulance. I wondered if alcohol always made her so energetic.

Sammy flushed at the mention of her breakup. Ryan looked at her as if he thought she was going to need to sit back down.

"Well, if that's cause for celebration, then congratulations, Sammy," Mike said hesitantly. As a Cape Bay native and a longtime regular at Antonia's, Mike should have known Sammy had been seeing Jared practically forever and that the breakup wasn't the easiest thing for her.

"Thanks," she said quietly.

Mike kept his eyes on her as he nodded. For a second, I thought he was going to walk away without asking me any more questions, but then he looked right at me. "So you were just walking by?"

"Actually," Dawn interrupted, oblivious to the fact that Mike was talking to me instead of her, "we were down at the Mexican place." She waved her arm wildly in the general direction of Fiesta Mexicana and almost smacked Mike in the face. "I overheard the table next to us talking about how somebody found a body down here, so I thought we should come and check it out."

"You heard there was a body, and your first thought was to come and investigate?" Mike asked Dawn, even though he was looking at me. I tried to keep my face perfectly neutral, even though I knew what he was getting at.

"Yeah, basically," Dawn replied. "Why not?"

"Fran?" Mike said, ignoring Dawn.

"It was Dawn's idea," I said, hearing how childish I sounded.

Mike stared at me stoically.

"I didn't want to come down here. I would have been perfectly happy keeping up with my margarita drinking. I've had enough dead bodies for a few decades."

"Have you now?"

Before I could respond, Sammy interrupted. "It was my fault. Dawn said they found the body next to Mary Ellen's, and I thought she might need some moral support. Fran really didn't want to come."

Mike looked from me to Sammy and back again. Then he lifted one hand and made a beckoning motion. "Come here a minute, Fran."

I followed him around to the front of the ambulance. He folded his arms across his chest and looked at me without saying anything.

I tried to wait him out, but I finally couldn't take it anymore. "Really, I just wanted to stay at the restaurant and hang out. We were supposed to be celebrating Sammy's breakup. I don't want anything to do with another body." It was true, but I couldn't blame him for being suspicious.

After each of Cape Bay's two recent murders, I'd done a little bit more investigating than Mike would have liked. Which was to say, he wanted me to stay out of it completely and leave all the investigating to the police. But it was hard when each of the cases directly affected friends of mine.

To my credit, I'd found the key evidence that led to the murderers' arrests in both cases. Mike didn't like to admit it, but if pressed, or if under the influence of a beer or two, he'd begrudgingly give me credit. I knew because his wife Sandra had told me.

Mike stared at me a few more seconds and then sighed heavily. "Just...try to stay out of it this time, okay?"

I nodded. "I'll do my best."

He eyed me and shook his head. "It's a suicide anyway. There's not much that needs investigating."

"That's good. For you, I mean. It's not good that someone's dead."

"Never is," Mike said and turned to walk away. He'd made it a few steps when I thought of something.

"Hey, Mike?"

He turned around, looking weary already. "Yeah?"

"Who was it?"

Mike paused for a second, and I felt tension grow in the pit of my stomach. Cape Bay was a small town, the kind of place where everybody knew everybody, if not by sight then by name. Everybody in this town was somebody's mother, son, girlfriend, husband, sibling, or best friend. Whoever's body was in the alley, somebody would be walking into my café tomorrow brokenhearted over it. I just didn't know if that person would be me.

"We don't know," he said finally.

I gasped. My mind went straight to the worst—that the body was unidentifiable.

"He's not a local," Mike said.

I almost burst into tears from relief.

"Nobody recognizes him. We're waiting for the ME's office to get here so we can move the body and check for a wallet."

"So he was a tourist?" I asked. My initial reaction of relief quickly shifted to concern as I realized that a vacationer getting shot in our town would be extremely bad for our tourism business. Not that that compared to how awful it would be for whoever he was vacationing with.

"Depends on whether you consider everyone from out of town to be a tourist. If you do, then yes. If you mean a vacationer, well, I don't know yet."

I looked at Mike curiously.

"He—" he started, then stopped and seemed to debate how much he wanted to tell me. I knew he thought giving me too much information would get me interested in the case, but I wasn't going near this one. I was done involving myself in police investigations. Finally, he gave in. "He wasn't dressed like a vacationer."

"No Hawaiian shirt and camera around his neck?" I asked, thinking of the most stereotypical tourist outfit I could. Of course, the last time I'd thought that, I'd been wrong, but it was still an outfit that screamed "Tourist!"

Mike chuckled. "No. More business casual."

Mike was right. Business casual clothes didn't sound much like what you packed for vacation.

"Mike!" someone called from somewhere in the direction of the alley.

"On my way!" Mike yelled back. He turned and looked at me. "Duty calls. Stay out of it, Fran, okay?"

"Trust me, Mike. I have no interest in this case."

He grunted and stalked off around the ambulance. I walked back over to Dawn and

Sammy, who were still huddled at the back of the ambulance. Ryan was gone, probably off to wherever Mike was.

"So you're not under arrest?" Dawn asked.

"No. Why would I be?" I retorted.

"We're at a crime scene, and a cop wanted to talk to you. Makes sense to me."

"It's not a crime scene," I said.

Dawn looked at me with the predictable "are you stupid?" look on her face that she seemed fond of giving me. "Um, the dead body over there would say different," Dawn said, after apparently deciding that my stupidity wasn't going to resolve itself.

"It was a suicide," Sammy said quietly. I could tell the sight of the body was still bothering her. Not that I could blame her. It was still bothering me, too.

"Well, whatever. What did ol' Officer Mike want?" Dawn asked.

"Nothing important," I said. I wasn't sure if Dawn knew about my involvement in the previous cases—it wasn't like the CBPD had broadcast the news that a civilian was solving their crimes—and I didn't want to fill her in now if she didn't.

"Telling you to stay out of it?" Apparently, Dawn did know.

"Maybe," I admitted.

Dawn laughed, a big, loud laugh. A couple of the officers turned around and gave her the eye. Laughing noisily probably wasn't the most tactful way to behave in the presence of a dead body.

"Maybe we should leave," I suggested.

"We haven't seen Mary Ellen," Sammy said.

As much as I didn't want to hang around any longer, Mary Ellen was the only reason we had come there in the first place. Leaving without seeing or talking to her would completely defeat the purpose of having left our comfortable seats on the patio of Fiesta Mexicana.

"Okay, let's go find her," I said.

"How are we going to do that in all this mess?" Dawn asked, gesturing at the crowd of people, cops, and police cars.

I knew Mary Ellen had only been an excuse for Dawn to get us to come there, and it annoyed me that she was trying to get out of seeing her now. "We just start looking," I said.

"Start with her store," Sammy said.

It was so blazingly obvious that I didn't know how I hadn't already thought of it. "Of course," I said. "Let's go." I started off through the crowd toward Mary Ellen's shop, with Sammy and Dawn trailing behind me.

Sammy hurried to catch up. "Did Mike say who it was?" she asked as quietly as she could in the noisy crowd of people.

I shook my head. "They don't know yet. Out-of-towner, they think."

Sammy nodded in acknowledgment as we walked to the front of Mary Ellen's shop. I don't know what I expected to see, but I was surprised all the lights were off. Logically, it made sense. It was long past closing time, and Mary Ellen wasn't the type to open just so tourists could come in to buy morbid mementos of the time a body was found in their vacation spot.

"It's all closed up," I said.

I wondered if maybe Mary Ellen had gone home and didn't need our moral support at all.

"I don't know if we'll be able to find her with all these people hanging around," Dawn said. "We could always go back to the restaurant and get our drink on. You guys can come find her tomorrow. Tonight was supposed to be about Sammy, after all." She bumped her denim-clad hip into Sammy's.

Sammy glared at her. "The light's on in the back," she said. I leaned toward the front window of the store and realized a light I'd thought was reflected from the street was actually coming from deep inside.

Dawn looked too. "She's probably back there with the cops or something."

Sammy rolled her eyes at Dawn and walked over to the glass door. She knocked on it rapidly, paused, and then knocked again. I watched the patch of light in the back to see if I could detect any movement.

Sammy had just raised her hand to knock again when I saw a head peek through the lit doorway. I put my hand on Sammy's shoulder to get her attention and then pointed to the head. She framed her eyes with her hands and leaned up against the glass.

"Mary Ellen? Mary Ellen!" she called through the door. "Mary Ellen!"

The owner of the head moved fully into the doorway. The person was completely backlit, so I couldn't be sure, but the hair looked an awful lot like Mary Ellen's.

"Mary Ellen!" Sammy called again. "It's me, Sammy! And Dawn and Fran."

The person began to move through the store toward us. When she finally reached the front of the store, the light from the street caught her face and her curly blond hair, and I saw it really was Mary Ellen. I breathed a sigh of relief. Even though I knew the body in the alley was a suicide, I was still a little creeped out and uneasy about a shadowy figure approaching us.

Mary Ellen unlocked the door, and Sammy stepped aside so she could push it open.

"Ladies, come in," she said, motioning us to enter.

Mary Ellen Chapman was older than the three of us, closer to my mother's age than mine, but still young enough to have been impossibly cool in my youthful eyes. For one thing, she was the only adult in town who had let us call her by her first name when we were children. She'd said if her first name was on the front of her store, there was no sense in the kids calling her "Mrs. Chapman."

As an adult, I wondered if it also might have had something to do with her being widowed shortly before she moved to Cape Bay. Maybe she didn't want to be reminded of her husband's death by constantly being addressed by her married name.

In any case, my mom and the other parents begrudgingly accepted us using her first name, as long as we put a "miss" in front of it. So she was "Miss Mary Ellen" all through my childhood and up until I graduated college, when I casually dropped it despite the glares I received from my mother as a result.

"Mary Ellen, we heard about the body and–" Sammy started as soon as we got inside.

"Let's go in the back," Mary Ellen interrupted. She locked the door behind us. "Too many strange ears out there."

I glanced over my shoulder as we followed her toward the back room, wondering who was out there that she didn't want overhearing our conversation.

Chapter Four

Mary Ellen invited us to sit down at the little table in the back room of her store. The space was bigger and far less crowded than the back room at my café. Shelves lined the wall, full of supplies and extra stock. A computer sat on the desk. Handmade jewelry was scattered across the table next to the desk, surrounded by four chairs.

"Sorry for the mess," Mary Ellen said. "I was just sorting through some new pieces one of the local jewelry designers brought in. Can I get you ladies anything?"

Sammy and I shook our heads. "No, thank you," we both said.

"You have any beer?" Dawn asked with a laugh.

"No, I don't." Mary Ellen pulled the last chair out from the table, but Dawn interrupted her before she could sit.

"Water, then."

Mary Ellen stopped mid-sit and pushed herself back up. As soon as she turned to walk to the little refrigerator under her desk, I shot Dawn a glare. She made a face at me. Mary Ellen brought a bottle of water to the table and placed it in front of Dawn. "Anything else I can get you?" she asked.

"No, this'll be fine, thanks," Dawn said.

I breathed a sigh of relief, grateful she hadn't decided to ask for a snack.

Mary Ellen sat down and spread her hands out on the table. She took a slow, deep breath as she stared blankly at a point somewhere in the middle of the table.

"How are you?" Sammy asked.

Mary Ellen turned her head toward Sammy, looking startled, as though she'd already forgotten we were there. "What was that, Sammy? Did you say something?"

"I asked how you're doing. You know, because of..." Sammy waved her hand in the direction of the alley.

Mary Ellen took a deep breath. "I'm fine. Certainly better than the fellow out there. I just..." She sighed heavily and shook her head, not bothering to finish the sentence.

Sammy reached out and took one of Mary Ellen's hands. Mary Ellen grasped it tightly. Her big blue eyes were tearful, and I thought she might erupt in sobs at any second. Not that I could blame her, given the circumstances.

"I'm sorry," Mary Ellen said. "It's just so hard to believe. Someone killed—so close—just steps away." She brought her other hand to her mouth and held it there for a second.

"Mary Ellen—" Sammy started, then stopped while she waited for Mary Ellen to look at her. "Mary Ellen, it wasn't murder. He killed himself."

Mary Ellen looked at Sammy with confusion in her eyes. She opened her mouth a couple of times as though she wanted to say something, but each time, she stopped herself, looking more confused than before. Finally, she managed to put a sentence together. "Is that what the police said?"

Sammy nodded. "There didn't seem to be any doubt."

Mary Ellen's eyes drifted away from Sammy's face. I couldn't tell what she was thinking, but she seemed troubled.

"Will you be all right alone here tonight?" Sammy asked. I was impressed by her compassion for Mary Ellen. It had been a deeply upsetting night, which was supposed to have been a celebration of Sammy's freedom. The way she put all that aside and concerned herself with only Mary Ellen's well-being made me proud to be her friend.

Mary Ellen's eyes widened, and she glanced out through the darkened store to the brightly lit street beyond. Her apartment was upstairs from the store.

All the shops on Main Street had apartments on the second floor, except the few that had been converted for another purpose—a studio for one of the local artisans, extra sales floor space for a downstairs shop, and a whole separate store.

When my grandparents had first moved to Cape Bay, they'd lived in the apartment above the café while they waited for children to come along. Mary Ellen had lived in the apartment above her own shop since she'd arrived in town twenty-five or so years earlier. Whatever was going on outside was impossible to ignore while she was sleeping–or trying to sleep–upstairs.

"Do you want me to stay with you tonight?" Sammy offered.

"No, tonight's supposed to be about you," I said. "Mary Ellen, I'll stay with you if you don't want to be alone."

"Fran, you have Latte to worry about. I'll stay," Sammy replied, referring to my beloved café-au-lait–colored Berger Picard dog. He was a stray I'd adopted a couple of months earlier after he found me in the park.

"He's with Matt," I said. "He can keep Latte overnight."

"It's fine–"

"Ladies!" Mary Ellen interrupted, stopping Sammy and me from debating the matter any further. I noticed Dawn hadn't jumped in at all. "Ladies, I am a grown woman, and I have been living on my own for twenty-five years. I certainly don't need one of you to stay here and babysit me just because there are a few police cars outside. And you said yourself, Sammy, there's no murderer on the loose that I need protecting from." She must have realized she was still clasping Sammy's hand because she dropped it quickly.

"Mary Ellen, really, I don't mind—" Sammy started.

"Any of us would be happy—" I said at the same time as Sammy.

Dawn made a face, which I was glad Mary Ellen hadn't seemed to see.

"Girls, I will be fine!" Mary Ellen said, emphasizing the word *girls* and, with it, how much younger than her we were.

Sammy gave me an imploring look, and I shrugged in response. If Mary Ellen didn't want us, we wouldn't be able to convince her otherwise.

"If you're sure..." Sammy said cautiously.

"I'm sure. I appreciate you all coming by to check on me, but I'll be fine on my own tonight. The doors all have locks, and besides, I have a feeling the police will be out there for half the night anyway." She nodded toward the street.

She was probably right. Mike and his team did seem to be taking their time.

"Would you like us to stay a while, or should we go?" Sammy asked.

"Don't ruin your night's fun for me," Mary Ellen said. "It sounds like you were having a bit of a girls' night. Is it your birthday, Sammy?"

"No—"

"We were celebrating her breakup with her loser boyfriend," Dawn said, finally finding something in the conversation she cared about.

"Jared?" Mary Ellen asked, looking surprised. "The two of you had been together for quite a while, hadn't you?"

"Ten years," Sammy said.

"Ten years too long!" Dawn interjected.

"And this is cause for celebration?" Mary Ellen asked.

"I guess," Sammy said at the same moment Dawn exclaimed, "Yes!"

"We wanted to show Sammy our support," I said to Mary Ellen. "And take her out to have some fun and get her mind off things."

"Well, don't let me stop you from going out and enjoying yourselves," Mary Ellen said.

"You heard the lady." Dawn stood up. "I can hear the margaritas calling me."

"We're not going back for more margaritas," Sammy said. "Well, I'm not, anyway. You're welcome to."

"Then what do you want to do? Go out to the bar? Go back to your place and make our own drinks? Find a movie with some hot shirtless guys we can watch?"

"I don't care what you do. I'm staying here with Mary Ellen if I can convince her to let me. Otherwise, I'm going home—by myself—and going to bed. I've had enough celebrating for tonight."

Dawn looked annoyed as she sat back down in her chair.

"Mary Ellen," Sammy said, looking over at her, "since you wouldn't be getting in the way of any celebrating, would you like us—me—to stay a while or go?"

Mary Ellen looked between us as if trying to decide whether she wanted any of our company. I wouldn't have blamed her if she'd asked us to go just for fear of Dawn staying. "Well, if you really want to stay, I could use some help getting this jewelry sorted and tagged for sale."

"I'd be happy to help out," Sammy said.

"If you don't mind, I'll stay, too," I said. "It'll give me a chance to look all this stuff over and figure out what I'm coming back to buy."

I recognized the jewelry on the counter as the work of Marti Bowman. She mostly worked with silver, making delicate filigree pieces I'd loved for years. My mother had made it a tradition to buy me a piece or two for every Christmas and birthday. Between those pieces and the ones I'd inherited after my mother's death, I had a fairly sizeable collection. That made me even more eager to see all her newest pieces.

Dawn withered and sank lower in her chair.

"You don't have to stay," Sammy said to her.

Dawn shrugged, and I silently wished for her to go. "I'll stay," she said. "I like Marti Bowman's stuff. It'll be cool to look through it."

I was surprised. I had been almost certain she wouldn't want to stay. But then I realized that if she was Sammy's best friend, they had to have something in common. Sammy was quiet and mostly a homebody, while Dawn was one of the most boisterous people I'd ever met, and she went out every chance she got. But they had to meet in the middle somewhere, and apparently tonight, that was the back room of Mary Ellen's shop.

Mary Ellen spread the jewelry out so we could reach it easily and dropped a pile of tags in the middle of the table with a price list. She explained briefly what she needed us to do, and the four of us settled in to get the jewelry ready for sale. As my grandmother would say, "Many hands make light work." It turned out to be surprisingly fun. We laughed and chatted as we sorted and tagged the pieces. Even Dawn perked up and seemed to enjoy herself, despite the lack of slushy, citrusy alcohol.

It took a little over an hour to finish everything Mary Ellen needed done.

"Thank you, ladies!" she said as we stood in the back room, getting ready to leave. "This would have taken me a week if I had to do it on my own. I'll set up the display in the morning. I know Marti will be happy it's out there so quickly."

"We're happy to help." Sammy smiled.

"I appreciate you giving up your girls' night out to do it." Mary Ellen leaned over to hug Sammy.

"To be honest, finding out the police were investigating a dead body kind of put a damper on things, so this was a good distraction," Sammy replied.

"For me, too."

We said our goodbyes and headed for the front door. We would normally have gone out the back instead of making our way through the darkened store, but we could tell by the spotlights still shining in through the plate glass windows that the police were still set up outside, so the alley would be closed.

Dawn and I had just stepped into the darkness of the store when Mary Ellen reached out and touched Sammy's arm.

"Oh, Sammy!" she said. "I have something for you." She turned to Dawn and me. "You two go on ahead. Just turn the bolt to unlock it. You know how to do it, Fran. It's the same as yours."

Dawn and I went ahead and waited on the sidewalk for Sammy. The entire CBPD was still milling around. Flashes of light came from the alley, where one of the officers was still taking pictures. A couple of the others were taking notes as they talked to people in the crowd. Mike and Ryan were huddled together near one of the police cars. I realized with relief that the ambulance was gone, along with the man under the sheet.

Sammy emerged from the store as Mary Ellen held the door open for her.

"Thank you again, ladies!" Mary Ellen called out with a wave. "Be careful going home." She waved again as she closed and locked the door then disappeared toward the back room.

"What did she have for you?" Dawn asked.

Sammy raised her hand to her throat and held out the sparkly bauble dangling there. It was a tiny three-dimensional heart made of intertwined silver-and-gold filigree, with the twisted silver-and-gold chain emerging from the center as though it were two strands. It was obviously one of Marti's pieces and one of the prettiest things I'd ever seen.

"It's called 'Full Heart,'" Sammy said. "Mary Ellen said she wanted me to have it as a reminder that my heart is whole, even without Jared."

"That's so sweet," I said.

"It's gorgeous. I'm jealous!" Dawn bumped her shoulder into Sammy's with a smile.

Sammy smiled back, looking the happiest I'd seen her since the breakup. I knew her well enough to know it wasn't the gift or its value that made her happy but the sentiment behind it.

We lingered for another minute or so, admiring Sammy's necklace and Mary Ellen's generosity, then made our way down the road toward Sammy's and Dawn's apartments.

They both lived in apartments above shops on Main Street. When I'd first found out they were best friends but didn't live together, I was a little surprised, but as I got to know them both better, I came to understand they were probably smart to live apart. They loved each other, but they wouldn't have lasted long sharing a living space.

We left Dawn at her apartment first then headed for Sammy's.

"Are you going to be all right walking home alone?" she asked when we reached her door.

"Sure, I'll be fine," I assured her.

"Really? I can drive you if you want."

"No, I'll be fine. Promise."

"Okay, if you say so." She hugged me. "Thanks for a good night."

I laughed. "I don't know if I really did much to make it a good night."

"You were there. That meant a lot."

"I'm glad I could be there for you."

I watched to make sure Sammy got in okay then headed for Matt's house on a road off Main Street. The street lights were shining, but after the brightness of the police spotlights outside Mary Ellen's, the road seemed dim and shadowed. Once I got onto my street, where the lights were spaced farther apart, I found myself walking a little faster.

"There's nothing to be afraid of," I told myself. "It was a suicide, not a murder. There's nothing to be afraid of." Still, the shadows seemed ominous.

Chapter Five

By the time I turned onto Matt's front walk, I was barely able to keep from breaking into a jog. I should have taken Sammy up on her offer to drive me home—if only so that anyone who happened to be looking out their window and saw me scamper by wouldn't think I had lost my mind. But then I remembered that Matt and I were the two youngest residents on a street mostly populated by people a generation older than we were.

Our neighbors seemed to go to bed at nightfall, so no one was likely to see me rushing by. That thought made me even more nervous, and I ran the last few steps to Matt's door. I rapped quickly on the door then grabbed the knob. It was locked, so I knocked again.

Matt pulled open the front door, and I flung myself into his arms.

"Matty!" I exclaimed, my childhood nickname for him bursting from my lips.

He hesitated for a moment then hugged me close.

"What's going on?" he asked, clearly confused. "Are you okay?"

Latte poked his nose at me, trying to figure out where my hands were and why they weren't scratching his head. Giving up, he popped up on his back legs and leaned his front legs against me. I released Matt and reached down to rub Latte's ears. Matt leaned out the door and looked around.

"You just miss me that much?" he asked after determining there was nothing outside.

I nodded, suddenly feeling silly for letting imagination run away with me. "Yeah, you and Latte. Latte mostly."

Matt cast another glance outside then closed the door. "How was your girls' night?"

"Okay." I walked into the dimly lit living room, with Latte following along. Matt had one of the late-night talk shows on TV. I walked to the kitchen and flipped on the light before glancing at the back door to make sure it was locked. I decided it was overkill to cross the kitchen and turn on the bathroom light just for the sake of soothing my overactive imagination. Instead, I grabbed a glass from the cabinet and went to the sink to pour myself a glass of water.

"Just okay?" Matt asked, standing in the entryway to the kitchen.

I nodded as I chugged the water then put the glass on the counter. "A little short."

Matt made a face and looked at the clock over the sink. "It's after midnight."

"Yeah, well..." I stopped and sighed.

Matt looked at me with his eyebrows raised. Tiny Cape Bay didn't have its own news broadcast, and the one from Boston had things to report other than the goings-on of a little resort town over an hour away. News travels fast in a small town, but mostly during daylight hours. Matt had no way of knowing about the interruption to Sammy's celebration.

"They found a body," I said.

"They *what?*"

"That's right—dead body."

"Who? Where?"

"I'm not sure who. In the alley next to Mary Ellen's store. Mike said it was a suicide."

"Mike was there?" Matt asked.

"Of course he was. You think no one called the police about a body in an alley?"

Matt shot me a dirty look. "Smart mouth," he muttered.

"You sound like my mother."

"I'll take that as a compliment."

I rolled my eyes. He always could get the better of me.

"Is that what you're so spooked about?" he asked.

"Spooked? I'm not spooked." Now that I'd had the chance to calm down in the bright light of Matt's kitchen, my earlier panic was starting to feel silly.

Matt's lips twitched, and his eyebrows rose. "Oh really? So you were just that happy to see me?"

"Mm-hmm." I nodded.

Matt shook his head. He knew I was trying to brush off my anxiety, but he was a good enough guy that he let me.

"You want to talk about it?" he asked.

I shook my head, shrugged, then nodded. "Maybe."

"Glass of wine?"

"Please."

Matt crossed the tiled floor and grabbed two wine glasses out of the cabinet. He pulled a bottle of red wine out of the rack. I handed him the corkscrew, and he popped the bottle open. He poured out two generous glasses and handed one to me.

He wedged the cork back in, picked up the bottle with one hand, took his wine glass in the other, and gestured toward the living room. I followed him, and Latte followed me.

Matt sat down on the far end of the couch, putting the wine bottle on the end table. I kicked off my shoes and curled up on the opposite side. Latte settled in between us, resting his paws on my feet. Though Latte obviously loved Matt, I never doubted that he was completely devoted to me.

"So somebody killed themselves in the alley next to Mary Ellen's store," Matt said.

I nodded.

"Weren't you going out for margaritas?"

I nodded again.

"Those two places are at least half a mile apart. How did a body at Mary Ellen's mess up your night out at Fiesta Mexicana?"

"Dawn."

Matt's forehead wrinkled. I could tell he was trying to figure something out, and I finally realized what it was.

"Sammy's friend. Dawn..." I paused while I tried to think of her last name. I still couldn't come up with it. "Dawn, Sammy's friend. Not sunrise dawn."

"Ohhh," Matt breathed, realization setting in. "Oh," he said again, this time in the same tone Mike had used. I had a feeling a lot of people used that tone when they realized Dawn was involved in something. It was remarkable how just telling people that I'd been with her explained how the whole night had gone off in an unanticipated direction.

I sipped my wine as he paused for a minute.

"So, she overheard someone talking in the restaurant about the police finding a body and then dragged you and Sammy over there to check it out?" he asked. I wasn't sure if he thought that was the most logical or most ridiculous possible course of events, but with Dawn, the most ridiculous was probably also the most logical.

"Yup, that's it."

"Really?" Matt asked. Apparently, he had been leaning toward the ludicrous end of the spectrum.

"Well, almost. We never did find out who found the body. Just that it was found."

"Semantics. I'm still right."

"Of course you are." I took another sip of my wine.

"I wonder who did find the body."

I shrugged.

"You said it was in the alley? Behind a dumpster or something?"

"Nope. Just in the middle."

"So you saw it?" Matt looked confused.

"Well, it was covered by a sheet. There wasn't much to see, except—" I remembered Dawn saying she thought she saw blood.

"Except?" Matt prompted.

I shook my head. "Nothing. There wasn't much to see."

"But you talked to Mike?"

"Yup."

"I bet he was happy to see you."

"You could say that," I said, trying not to choke on my wine or spit it across the couch at Matt.

His eyes twinkled. It didn't take any great imagination for him to guess how Mike felt about seeing me anywhere near a dead body.

"What did he say?" Matt asked.

"Just told me to stay out of it," I said. "But it's a suicide. There's nothing to stay out of."

"And they thought my dad's death was natural."

I narrowed my eyes and looked at him. "What are you saying?"

He shrugged and sipped his wine. "Just that things aren't always the way they seem at first."

"You want me to get in trouble with Mike, don't you?" I poked at him with the foot Latte wasn't lying on. Latte snuggled closer to me.

Matt laughed and batted my foot away. "No, I'd actually prefer you didn't. I was just saying."

"Just saying what? Huh? Huh? Just saying what?" I kept poking at him determinedly.

He kept swatting my foot away. "Just saying you should stop doing that before I spill my wine all over the couch!"

I pulled my foot back and tucked it under me. "Good point. That would be a terrible end for good wine." I took another sip. "This is good wine, by the way. Where'd you get it?"

He told me, and we debated for a few minutes which places nearby had the best selection. After we'd come to a consensus, Matt topped off our glasses.

"So did Sammy enjoy the part of the girls' night she did get to have?"

"She seemed to. I mean, she's still feeling kind of sad, but I think she's starting to cheer up a little."

"The breakup was her idea, right?"

"Well, I think it was Dawn's idea, but Sammy's the one who did the actual breaking up."

"Dawn." Matt shook his head.

"Sammy actually said it was partly me, too, because I asked her why she was still with him if he treats her so poorly."

"Fran," Matt said in the same tone he'd used earlier, shaking his head again. I poked him with my foot. "Remind me to never take you go-karting for our anniversary."

"Remind me not to date you for ten years with no sign of commitment."

"Oh, that might be a problem," Matt said. "I wasn't planning on showing any signs of commitment until I'm at least forty."

"That's only six years away."

"Are we that old?" he asked.

"Yup, thirty-four," I replied.

"Wow, when did that happen?"

"Almost a year ago."

"I'm getting old, man. No wonder I've been getting so sore from all that working out I've been doing. See? This spot, right here." He slid the sleeve of his T-shirt up on his wine-holding arm to show me the increasing definition of the muscles there. "All those weights I've been lifting are hard on an old body." He'd been going to the gym lately and liked to point out its effects to me.

I liked to tease him and downplay it. "I don't think lifting a wine glass from your leg to your lips counts as lifting weights."

"It does if you keep it as full as I do." He poured more wine into each of our glasses. "So what was it that had you so spooked earlier?" he asked after we spent a few minutes watching the late night show's new host interview some B-list celebrity about his awful-looking movie premiering that weekend.

I shrugged as I debated whether I should 'fess up or keep playing it off. Matt probably wouldn't let it go until I told him the truth, so I decided to get it over with. "It's stupid," I said, then waited to see if he would pursue it.

He did, of course. "When I was six, I got scared because I found my dad's car doors locked. I was scared of locked car doors. Since my dad never locked his doors, I was convinced that meant there was somebody hiding in the trunk who had locked them to throw us off. You can't tell me that whatever scared you was stupider than that."

"You were a kid. Kids are allowed to be stupid."

"It was five years ago."

I laughed even though I was pretty sure I actually remembered that happening when we were kids. Unless it was an oddly persistent fear, I doubted it had happened that recently. Still, it made me feel a little bit better.

"I'm not really sure why I was so on edge," I said. "I think it was just seeing the body and then walking home alone in the dark. The streetlights aren't very bright out there. There's no one out on the street. Most of the time, it's great how quiet Cape Bay is. When you get scared about something, though, suddenly every shadow seems sinister, like there's someone lurking where you can't see them. At least in New York, there were enough people around that you could pretend someone would come help you if you were attacked."

Matt laughed.

"You said you wouldn't laugh!"

"I never said that," he replied. "But I wasn't laughing at you being afraid. I was laughing at you not even trying to pretend someone would actually come help you in New York."

"It's true."

"I know it is. That's why it's funny."

I shook my head and turned my attention back to the late night show. There was some band on I'd never heard of. Based on how they sounded, I wouldn't have minded never hearing them. They sounded like a lot of loud noise. I felt very old.

"Man, these guys suck," Matt said.

"You're not kidding."

"Apparently, they're very popular with the preteen girls, though."

I turned my head slowly from the TV to Matt, and my eyebrows shot up about as far as they could go. "I was not aware you spent a lot of time with preteen girls."

"A guy I work with took his daughter and a bunch of her friends to one of their concerts. He said he could barely hear the next day from all the high-pitched screaming in his ears."

"Was that from the girls or the band?" I asked as the lead singer launched into the screeching falsetto of the song's chorus.

"You know, I'm actually not sure," Matt said, rubbing his ear.

The song and the show finally ended, and the next one came on. I pretended to pay attention to the host's monologue, but my mind kept drifting back to the body in the alley. Something about it—besides the obvious—was bothering me, but I couldn't quite figure out what.

"What?" Matt asked, staring at my face intently.

"What?" I asked back.

"You look like you're trying to solve the Hodge conjecture."

"The what?"

"Never mind, it's a math thing. You look like you're thinking about something."

"Nothing in particular," I said, turning back to the TV. Well, nothing I could put my finger on, anyway. Whatever it was that was bothering me was still lurking at the edge of my brain, just beyond what I could consciously comprehend. I tried not to focus on it.

Just as the monologue ended and the band broke into the generic glorified hold music they all played, it came to me. I inhaled sharply.

"What?" Matt asked, looking at me as though he thought something was wrong.

"Matty, I don't think the man in the alley killed himself."

Chapter Six

"Franny!"

I wasn't sure whether Matt was annoyed or amused by my declaration. He was clearly surprised.

"What?" I tried to sound neutral.

"The one thing Mike told you to do was stay out of it."

"I know, but then I started thinking about it..."

Matt smiled and shook his head. At least he wasn't annoyed.

"You're the one who said things aren't always what they seem."

"It wasn't a suggestion to go looking."

"I know. I just—something about it was bothering me, and I couldn't figure out what it was."

"Maybe that someone killed himself in an alley?"

"I don't think he killed himself, remember?"

Matt rolled his eyes. "So, what then?" he asked. "Dropped dead and managed to make it look like a suicide just to throw off the cops? Or, oh God, you think it was murder, don't you?"

I looked away from him, not trying very hard to hide the fact that I did, indeed, think it was murder. The wine was making me feel a little silly.

"You really can't leave it alone, can you?"

I smiled and shrugged.

"So what was it? What got you thinking?"

"He had a bag," I said.

"A bag? A bag means he didn't kill himself?"

"It does when it's a bag of souvenirs."

Matt eyed me. "He had a bag of souvenirs?"

"Yup. From Mary Ellen's." I had seen the bag lying on the pavement next to the sheet-covered body. Its logo had looked familiar, but it wasn't immediately obvious where it was from. If it had been Mary Ellen's old logo, the one she'd had when she opened up her shop, I would have recognized it instantly. But she had recently put a new design on her business cards, ads, and bags she put her customers' purchases in. Her graphic designer niece had created it—clean and modern with Mary Ellen's initials intertwined in a swirl. It looked good, but I wasn't used to it yet. That little thing had prickled at the back of my mind. When I finally placed the logo, a red flag waved high in the air.

"So a bag of souvenirs means he didn't commit suicide?"

"Well, yeah. Why would you buy a bag full of souvenirs and then walk straight outside and kill yourself?"

"Your family would still get the stuff. The police don't keep it forever."

"Well, yeah, but why would you risk..." I thought back to the sight in the alley and lowered my voice before I continued, even though we were the only two people in the house. "Why would you risk getting blood on everything?"

"There was blood?"

I hesitated and made a face. "I'm not sure. There was a gun, though. I saw that." I realized the gun was the other thing bothering me—the violence of it. It wasn't just the loss of life but how aggressively it had been taken. That someone could do that to another person, or even to them-selves, upset me more than the death itself.

Matt grimaced. I could tell he hadn't put much thought into the *how* of the death until that moment. "I guess maybe you're right," he said.

"So you agree? You think it was murder?"

"I didn't say that. I said you had a point about the souvenirs."

"Thank you." I sipped my wine.

"But are you sure there were souvenirs in the bag? Did you actually see them or just the bag?"

I rested my glass against my lower lip. I wasn't sure. I only saw the outside of the bag. Anything could have been in that bag. So my theory wasn't as sound as I'd thought, but the bag from Mary Ellen's shop was full of—something or other. Souvenirs made the most sense, but that wasn't the most logical possibility. "I only saw the bag," I admitted. "But when we saw her, Mary Ellen was acting so strange."

"You talked to Mary Ellen?"

"Yeah. I didn't tell you that?"

"Nope."

"Sorry." I shook my head in an attempt to gather my thoughts. "I'm all over the place, aren't I?"

"It's okay." Matt reached out his sock-covered foot and rubbed it against my bare one. "You've had a rough night." He rested his foot on mine. Between him and Latte, my toes were toasty warm.

"The whole reason we actually went to the scene was to check on Mary Ellen. Sammy thought she might be upset and we should check on her. She was upset, but even more than I expected. She seemed—rattled."

Matt didn't say anything, but I could guess what he was thinking from the look on his face. It made just as much sense for Mary Ellen to be rattled by a suicide as a homicide.

"I don't know. Maybe I'm wrong. But something about that scene just didn't feel like a suicide."

Matt looked at me, his face twitching slightly as though he wanted to say something but was doing his best to hold back.

"Go ahead."

"As soon as I say this one thing, I'm going to tell you to go with your gut and go talk to Mary Ellen. See if the guy had been in her shop and find out why she seemed so upset about it. But first, I just have to ask: do you really think your instinct on this is more likely to be right? I mean, better than the instinct of a cop who has as much experience as Mike does?" Matt paused to let the question sink in then smiled. "But if you really feel strongly about this, you know, Franny, you should just go."

I smiled back at him. I knew he thought I was crazy for even considering that I might have caught onto something the police hadn't, but beyond a cautious warning or two, he wasn't going to say anything about it. He tolerated me investigating murders, and I tolerated him spending so much time watching football and baseball.

"I don't know," I said. "Maybe Mike was trying to keep it quiet. Maybe he was tired and didn't notice. Maybe I have a sixth sense for these things and should become a detective. Or a private eye. Or a psychic."

Matt laughed. "I think maybe you've had enough to drink."

I looked into my glass. "Nope, still some in there."

"Still some in the bottle, too." Matt reached for the wine bottle and poured the last of it into our glasses.

"I will take your suggestion, though."

Matt wrinkled his forehead, apparently having forgotten what he'd just said. I wondered if the wine was hitting him, too.

"To talk to Mary Ellen," I clarified. "I'll go by her shop tomorrow before I go to work and see if I can find anything out."

"Sounds like a plan." Matt stifled a yawn.

I looked at the cuckoo clock, which had belonged to Matt's mother and had hung in the same spot for as long as I could remember. Over the summer, Matt, like me, had moved back into the house where he'd grown up, and neither of us had redecorated. Not that the clock would move even if Matt did redecorate—his mom had died when we were kids, and I knew the clock was a special memento of her, which told me it was almost two in the morning.

"I better get going. You had to work today. You must be exhausted."

Matt stifled another yawn. "I'm fine. We can keep talking." He looked pitiful and adorable. The lids of his big brown eyes were heavy, and his dark hair was every bit as messy as I would have expected since he was going on twenty hours of awake time.

"No, I think I'm all talked out."

"You sure? I don't mind."

"I believe you, but I think you might fall asleep on me if I try to keep you up much longer."

"Me? No. I'm really okay." He closed his eyes and leaned his head against the back of the couch.

I pulled my foot out from where it was still tucked under his and kicked him.

"Ow!" he cried, popping his head back up.

"Walk me home." I wiggled my toes until Latte moved off my other foot. I stood up, stretched, then downed what was left of my wine. Matt finished off his glass and handed it to me. I took them to the kitchen, rinsed them out, and left them in the sink. Matt was barely pulling himself up off the couch as I put my shoes back on and started for the door.

"Hold up." He slowly got to his feet. "I'm coming." He shuffled over to the door, where he had a pair of slippers, and slid them on over his socks.

I looked at him in his warm-up pants, T-shirt, socks, and slippers, and shook my head. "You look like an old man."

"It's this street. This is how I see everybody dressed when they go out to get their papers in the morning, and I start to think this is how everyone dresses."

"In that case, you're missing your robe."

"You're right." He made a move for the bedroom.

"No!" I grabbed his arm to hold him in place, and he grinned at me. I knew he was just messing with me, but I also knew he wouldn't hesitate to actually wear the robe to walk me home. Then he could tease me about the time he walked me home in a robe after I said he looked like an old man, probably for the rest of my life.

Matt hooked Latte's leash to his collar. The leash was just a formality. Neither of us was likely to actually hold onto it. Only one house stood between Matt's and mine, and Latte knew the way home. Matt and I could stand on our respective front steps, and Latte would run between us if we told him to.

The three of us stepped outside. Matt didn't lock his door because it was Cape Bay, and our neighbors thought it was strange the two of us locked our doors when we went to work each day. Except, apparently, for murder, Cape Bay was a safe town.

Looking out at the street, I remembered how anxious I'd been walking to Matt's. The shadows were every bit as creepy right then as they had been before. Matt slipped his hand into mine, and we cut across our neighbor's lawn just as we'd done as kids. We had always said there was no sense in going all the way to the sidewalk when we could save a few steps. Our parents had disagreed, but the Williams family who lived in the house in between us never seemed to mind. So as long as our parents weren't looking, we would beeline across the grass.

Mr. and Mrs. Williams—I never could bring myself to call them by their first names, even though they'd assured me it was fine—still lived in the house, though I hadn't seen much of them since my return to Cape Bay. I'd seen even less of their son, Chase, though he came into the café from time to time.

He always seemed to come in when we were completely slammed, and I couldn't steal away to talk to him for even a few minutes. The best I could manage was a fond hello, a "What can I get you?" and a "Here you go!" He was a couple of years younger than I was, so he'd never been much of a playmate, but he was still someone I thought of with fondness when I looked back on my school years. I'd known one of his older sisters a little better because she was only a year older than me, but I hadn't so much as laid eyes on either her or her older sister since I left for college. They both had moved away, one to Boston and one to San Francisco. I would have to ask Chase or his mom how they were doing the next time I saw one of them.

We reached my front door, and I unlocked it then reached inside to flip on the light. Matt held my hand as Latte trotted over behind the big oak in the yard to take care of business.

"Are you sure you're going to be all right tonight?" he asked.

I nodded. "Yup, I'm sure." A little tightening in my abdomen made me wonder if he was fishing for me to invite him inside, but then I remembered how he'd almost fallen asleep on the sofa just five minutes earlier and decided he was just asking because he was a nice guy. Besides, if that's what he wanted, he could have asked me to stay instead of walking me home.

In any case, I wasn't sure if I was ready for that. I wasn't looking for any more emotional turmoil. Even though Matt was taking me to Italy with the money he'd made from the sale of his previous house, we had agreed to take things slow. We'd been friends for a long time, and neither of us wanted to mess up our friendship by getting too serious too fast.

"Okay, well, lock your doors, and don't worry about waking me up if you get scared and want to call me. I can be down here in about ten seconds, and if I run really fast, my robe will fly out behind me, and you'll feel like Superman is coming to your rescue."

"Yeah, well, you might want to trade those slippers for some sneakers unless you're actually planning on going flying through the air. Those things don't look like they have much traction."

Matt slid his foot back and forth across the surface of the step. "You may be right. I'll put my sneakers by the door. Or maybe I'll just run over barefoot. Isn't that supposed to be good for your knees or something?"

"I don't think it matters that much when you're running a couple hundred feet across grass."

"Then I'll just pick whichever's fastest."

I smiled. "You do that."

Latte ran past me into the house. I heard him lapping up his water in the kitchen, then he came back, nudged my hand, and went to stand on the stairs leading up to my bedroom.

"Looks like somebody's ready for bed," I said.

"That makes two of us."

"I thought you said you weren't tired!"

"I never said that. I said I would stay up and talk to you if you wanted. That just means I'm a good boyfriend, not that I'm not tired."

"Ah, I see."

Matt pulled me toward him. "Goodnight, Franny." He kissed me softly.

"'Night, Matty." I smiled.

He leaned around me and looked at Latte on the stairs. "Goodnight, my furry friend."

Latte blew out his breath and licked away some droplets of water that were clinging to his nose.

"I'll take that as a goodnight." He pulled me in for another quick kiss then released my hand and stepped off the front step. "I'll see you tomorrow."

"See you." I turned and went inside, locking the door behind me. I knew Matt wouldn't leave until he knew I was safely inside with the metaphorical hatches battened down.

I patted my leg as I stepped past Latte on the stairs, beckoning him to follow me. He trotted after me obediently. In my bedroom, he jumped onto my bed and flailed around, trying to get the quilt arranged to his liking. He stopped, and I thought he had everything the way he wanted it, but then he flailed again, rolled over, and flailed some more before he finally calmed down and rested his head on the spare pillow. The bed was a mess, but at least he was comfortable.

I changed my clothes, lay down, and turned out the light. Latte floundered around until his body was pressed against mine. I reached out to pet him, and he snuggled into me. In a few minutes, his slow, steady breathing told me he had fallen asleep. I tried to close my eyes, but they seemed determined to pop back open. Despite the ridiculously late hour and all the wine I'd drunk, my mind raced, and sleep eluded me. I couldn't stop thinking about what was in the bag lying beside the dead man and whether it would convince me more or less his death wasn't a suicide.

Chapter Seven

Latte nudged me awake far earlier than I would have liked given my late bedtime, but as soon as I was awake, there was no going back. The small part of my mind that had actually woken up went straight back to the dead man in the alley.

I pulled myself from bed. Latte perched on the edge of it, his eyes trained on me, watching and waiting for me to make a move toward the stairs. I could practically hear his little doggie thoughts: "Food. Food. Food. Food. Food. Food. Food. Food."

I rubbed my hands over my face a few times, reached back, and pulled the elastic out of my hair. The thick mass of dark waves fell down my back. I glanced in the mirror over the dresser. I hadn't realized how long my hair had gotten. I'd have to find time to get it cut. I didn't even know where to go. There was a salon down the street from my café. It had been there for about ten years, but I'd been in New York all that time and didn't know if it was any good. I'd have to ask Sammy about it.

I gave my scalp a quick massage and then pulled my hair back into a tight chignon. I changed into a T-shirt and a pair of flared yoga pants suitable for taking Latte on his morning walk and headed downstairs. Latte seemed to teleport from the bed to his bowl in the kitchen. He sat eagerly with one paw in the air, looking ready to explode with excitement. I scooped his food from the container in the pantry and refilled his water bowl as he practically inhaled the kibble.

When he was finished, he ran to the front door, picked up his leash, and resumed his "I can hardly wait" stance. I made him wait until my coffee was ready, not out of cruelty but because he probably wouldn't want me passing out halfway through our walk.

When my coffee was ready and safely poured into my travel mug, I grabbed his tennis ball and headed out. I was tempted to deviate from our normal path along the tree-lined residential streets and head to Main Street just to see if there was any activity in the alley next to Mary Ellen's, but Latte was a creature of habit, and he guided me to the left instead of the right. Just as well. I'd be seeing the alley later when I went to talk to Mary Ellen anyway.

My mind wandered as we walked. My thoughts predictably went straight to the body in the alley. Who was he? How had he died? Was it murder or suicide? Whichever one it was, why was the body right in the middle of the alley? Wouldn't it make more sense to hide in a corner somewhere? Why kill yourself, or someone else, practically out in the open where anybody walking by could have seen? Why didn't anybody see? Or did someone?

I found myself walking faster, leading Latte instead of letting him walk ahead of me like I normally did. We were almost past the park when I felt a tug at the leash and realized he had stopped to stare longingly at the fenced-in expanse of grass that served as the rec league playing fields and dog park.

Miraculously, at this hour on a beautiful weekend morning, the fields were empty. I wondered whether it was an oversight or a mix-up in scheduling. Or maybe there was a reason unknown to single, childless women like me why there were absolutely no sports being played on the fields on this particular Saturday morning.

But it didn't really matter why the fields were empty, just that they were. As distracted as I was by the body, and as anxious as I was to go talk to Mary Ellen about it, I couldn't say no when Latte looked at me with those sad puppy dog eyes.

We crossed the street into the park and headed into the enclosed fields. I made sure the gate was closed behind me then hurled the ball as far as I could across the grass. Latte took off like a shot, his little legs going so fast that it almost looked as though he were flying.

I chuckled as I thought about the night before when I'd warned Matt he would probably go flying if he tried to run across the grass to my house wearing his slippers. I could just see it—Matt running, his robe flapping in the air, his foot slipping, and him falling ungraciously into the bushes. In my scenario, he wouldn't have any injuries beyond a few scratches from the holly bush and the more significant one to his pride. I actually giggled as I thought it over.

Latte brought the ball back and dropped it at my feet. I tried not to cringe when I picked it up and drool covered my hand. I threw the ball and wiped my hand off on my shirt even though I knew it would be wet again as soon as Latte brought the ball back. I couldn't bring myself to just stand there with a drooly hand while I waited to throw the ball.

My thoughts were light for the rest of our playtime. We played chase a little bit. The game started out with Latte running behind me and ended up with him sprinting back and forth across the field as I trailed behind. From my understanding, the family Latte had lived with before I adopted him had kids, and I had a feeling his love of chase was from time spent running around with them. Those little legs of his could really go, and my sneakers kept slipping in the dew-covered grass. Matt really would have gone flying if he'd tried to run in his slippers.

When Latte finally lay down in the grass, panting heavily, I picked up his leash so we could walk back home. His fatigued pace kept me from moving too fast, even though my mind was back on Mary Ellen and the mystery of the body in the alley. I wondered if Mike felt this way when he was on a case, as if every mundane life task was spent preoccupied with pondering the questions of a murder—or suicide, as the case may be.

Latte and I got home, and I left him to drink his water and sprawl out on the cool tile floor while I went upstairs to shower and get dressed. I thought about making myself a quick brunch but decided I would just grab a sandwich at the café. I tried to get Latte to go outside. He stared up at me from the floor as if I had lost my mind, so I bent down and scratched him behind the ears.

"I'm going to work now, but I'll be back to check on you in a little bit, okay? You're a good boy, aren't you? Yes, you are! Yes, you are! Mommy loves you!" I'd had the dog barely a couple of months, and I was already baby-talking him. I would have been embarrassed, but I was devoted to him to the point that I didn't care what anyone else thought. I kissed him on his little doggie nose and headed out.

It was a short walk to Mary Ellen's, down the street and then up a few blocks. I arrived at the alley in a matter of minutes.

All signs of the previous night's events were gone. No police tape, evidence markers, or stains on the pavement. Nothing at all to indicate a man's body had lain there twelve hours earlier. Not even a bouquet of flowers to memorialize him. To me, that was even more tragic—no one seemed to miss the man at all. Unless, of course, the people who would miss him didn't know about his death yet—or they were the ones who'd killed him.

I walked past the alley and paused in front of Mary Ellen's. If I went into her store, I would be deliberately disregarding Mike's direction to stay out of it. Did I want to do that? Did I really want to get involved?

"Curiosity killed the cat," I heard my mother's voice say in my head.

"But satisfaction brought it back," I whispered in response. I pushed the door open, the bell overhead jingling to announce my presence. Mary Ellen, normally the type to greet a customer as soon as they walked in, didn't appear. "Mary Ellen?" I called. "Mary Ellen?"

My overactive imagination ran away with me, and I started worrying that Mary Ellen had been felled by whatever villain had killed the man in the alley. I glanced around for a weapon.

"Hi! How can I help you?" Mary Ellen called, emerging from the back room. A smile spread across her face when she spotted me. "Oh, hello, Francesca."

"Hi, Mary Ellen. How are you?"

"I'm well, and yourself?"

I waited a moment for her to register that I wasn't just politely trying to exchange idle pleasantries. I had been there the night before and knew how upset she'd been.

She sighed when she finally realized. "I've been better."

"I can imagine. Do you have a minute to talk?"

Mary Ellen motioned around the shop. "Saturday mornings aren't a very busy time for me. Most people come get their souvenirs before roll-over day." All the weekly vacation rentals rolled over on Saturdays. With the previous week's renters going out and the following week's renters coming in, it made sense that everyone would get their souvenirs before the day they were desperately trying to beat the traffic out of town.

"We usually get slammed for about two hours on Saturday mornings—everybody trying to get coffee before they hit the road. In fact, it's probably pretty crazy over there right now."

"Sammy holding down the fort?"

"Yup. Becky and Amanda were scheduled to work, too, so she's got plenty of helping hands."

"You can't fit much more than three people behind the counter, can you?"

"Not if anyone wants to be able to move."

Mary Ellen chuckled. "Ah, well, why don't you come into the back with me, and we can chat?"

I followed her to the back and took the same chair I'd sat in the night before. The table was now covered in an assortment of knitted items. I picked up an impossibly soft scarf and ran my hands over it.

"Did you make this?" I asked, knowing she was an accomplished knitter.

"I did," she said proudly. "Do you like it?"

"It's beautiful. Even nicer than some of the stuff I saw in Bergdorf's back in New York City."

"Oh, I doubt that."

"No, really! I'd swear it was cashmere."

"That's probably because it is," Mary Ellen said. "Would you like a cup of tea?" She poured tea from the kettle she had sitting on a hot plate into a mug decorated with a beach scene and "Cape Bay!" in a scrawling script.

"No thanks, I'm fine."

She eased herself into a chair to my right from which she could see out into the shop in case anyone came in. "So what did you want to talk about? Is it safe to guess you have your investigator's cap back on?"

Did everybody in town know about that? "Well, I wouldn't go as far as that. It's just been on my mind. It's so mysterious. Who was he? What was he doing in Cape Bay? Why would he kill himself practically out in the open like that?" I stopped and shook my head. "I don't know. It just bothers me."

Mary Ellen nodded and shifted in her chair. "Death is upsetting," she muttered as she raised her mug to her lips.

I studied her for a moment. I suspected her mid-length curly blond hair got both its color and texture from a bottle. She didn't wear much makeup, just a little around her eyes and a touch of red on her lips. She'd aged well for the most part. Other than a few scattered wrinkles, she looked almost exactly as she had when she'd first arrived in town. But at that moment, there was something else in her eyes—a guardedness, perhaps? Sadness? Fear?

"Were you here when the man, uh, died?"

"I was," she said simply.

I waited for her to elaborate, but she didn't. I'd hoped it would be easier to get her to volunteer information without much prompting, but our conversation didn't seem to be going that way. "Did—did you hear it?" I asked, lowering my voice as though that would somehow make my question less horrifying.

She fixed her pale-blue eyes on me for a second, her mug held in both hands at her mouth, then shifted her gaze back to the door. Her head bobbed in the slightest nod.

"It was a gunshot?"

She paused then flicked her eyes to me, a scant smile playing at her lips. "For someone who's not investigating, you certainly have a lot of questions."

I blushed and looked down at the scarf I was still absently petting. "Mike told me to stay out of it."

"I haven't stayed single for a quarter century by obediently doing whatever a man tells me to do. Now tell me what you really want to know."

I looked at her, silently trying to judge whether she was really going to answer my questions just on the basis of female solidarity. Based on her expression and my previous experience, I decided she probably was, so I went straight to my real questions.

"When I—briefly—saw the body in the alley, I saw a bag on the ground next to it. A bag with a bunch of stuff in it that looked like it was from your store."

Mary Ellen nodded.

"Did he come in here?"

She nodded again.

"Just before he died?"

A third nod.

"Tell me."

She took a deep breath and a sip of her tea. "It was just before closing. He came in, looked around a while, gradually selected some items, paid, left, and died."

Well, that was one way to say it. I tried to think like a cop. What would Mike ask?

What had Mike probably already asked when he had surely interviewed Mary Ellen himself? "What did he buy?"

"Oh, a bunch of things. A couple of those little key chains we have—the cheap, plastic ones, not the nice metal ones—a pair of earrings, a little stuffed bear, some of the Mason jar soups Sue Hodges makes, some marzipan, and, uh, I think that's it."

My mouth started watering at the mention of soup and marzipan. Sue's Mason jar soups were perfect single-size servings of a wide variety of classic soups—chicken, tomato, vegetable, and, of course, New England clam chowder—that she made at home, pressure canned, and sold in a few local shops. They were divine.

And the marzipan! Mary Ellen got it from a local pastry shop. It was sweet and almondy and came in the cutest shapes.

There were the plain square-shaped, chocolate-covered ones, of course, but there were also flowers, hearts, and every kind of animal I could imagine. The designs were only limited by the skill of the person molding the dough. My favorites were the fruit and vegetable shapes. Biting into something that looked exactly like a tiny banana, carrot, or lime but tasted like candy always made me happy.

The thought made me hungry. I hadn't eaten breakfast, and it was creeping up on lunchtime. If I could have raided Mary Ellen's display case right then, I could have put away ten or so of those little candies.

"Francesca?"

"Hmm?" I looked up to see Mary Ellen looking at me expectantly.

"Are you there?" She smiled. "You look like you're a thousand miles away."

"Oh, sorry. I got distracted by the marzipan. Skipped breakfast this morning."

Mary Ellen chuckled and stood up. She walked to a shelf and pulled down a plastic container. She brought it over to me and opened it. Inside were about four dozen tiny marzipan figures, and most of them were the fruits and vegetables I adored.

"Oh, no, I'm fine. Really." I couldn't take my eyes off the perfectly crafted little apple at the top of the container. A little leaf with delicate veins etched into it sprouted from the stem.

"Take it!" Mary Ellen pushed the plastic box closer to me.

Reluctantly, I took a piece of candy and sank my teeth into it. It was every bit as good as I'd hoped.

"So was that all you wanted to know? What the gentleman bought?"

"No." I swallowed. "Although I am impressed that you remembered all those things he bought."

Mary Ellen shrugged her slender shoulders. "He turned out to be a rather memorable customer."

"I can see how that would happen." I certainly would remember every detail about an encounter with a customer who died moments after stepping outside of my café. "Was he here with anyone?"

Mary Ellen shook her head.

"Did you see anyone outside?"

She shook her head again.

"Did you hear anything before the gunshot?"

Mary Ellen paused and then nodded.

I took a deep breath. I was about to find out something very important or be very annoyed. "What did you hear?"

"I heard the man yelling. I couldn't understand all of it, but he was saying 'no' to someone. I don't know who. I didn't see. There was more yelling and then the gunshot. I didn't go out to look. I didn't even go to the door to lock it. I just closed myself in the back room and called the police."

I didn't blame her. No wonder she'd looked so shaken. I picked up a tiny marzipan carrot, complete with leafy stems. "So there was definitely someone else out there? You heard them?"

"Yes. Well—"

"What is it?"

"Like I said, I never actually saw anyone. And I heard yelling, but I don't know if it was one voice or two. I can't be certain."

"Is there anything else, Mary Ellen? Anything you saw or heard that might not have seemed significant at the time? Anything at all?"

She thought for a moment as I nibbled on my "carrot," feeling a bit like Bugs Bunny. Finally, she shook her head. "No, that's all."

I was disappointed. I don't know what I'd hoped—maybe for Mary Ellen to tell me exactly who the dead man was. Who killed him and why. But all I'd gotten was confirmation he'd been in her store and bought souvenirs right before he died.

"I'm sorry I can't be of more help, dear."

"It's fine, Mary Ellen." I smiled. "I appreciate you talking to me. And the marzipan. I could eat this stuff all day."

"Well then, why don't you take some with you?"

"No, no, it's fine. I've had plenty."

"It's on the house, Fran. I'm not going to charge you for a little box of marzipan."

"I was actually thinking of buying a jar or two of soup anyway."

"Just take them. Consider it a thank you for you girls coming to check on me last night. I do appreciate it."

Mary Ellen put a small assortment of the marzipan figures into a box. She put the candy and the soups I'd picked out into a bag and handed it to me. I was halfway to the door when a thought crossed my mind.

"Mary Ellen, the souvenirs the man bought last night—how did he pay for them?"

"By credit card."

My heart pounded. I took a breath. "A real credit card? Not a gift card? Did it have his name on it?"

"Yes."

Chapter Eight

I took a deep breath. Mary Ellen had the most important piece of information in the case so far, and she hadn't volunteered it. Had she told the police? Had Mike known who the dead man was when I'd talked to him the night before? Was there a reason he was keeping that information to himself? Was there a reason Mary Ellen hadn't told me?

"What was his name, Mary Ellen?"

"Abraham Casey."

"Are you sure?"

"Of course I'm sure! I'll never forget that man's name or his face." She walked to the cash register and punched a few buttons to open it. She pulled out a receipt and handed it to me. "See? Abraham Casey."

I took the receipt and studied it. Abraham Casey's signature was a mess, the way a doctor's looks on a prescription pad. He'd signed his name with an A, squiggles, a C, and more squiggles, including one that dropped below the signature line. I gave the receipt back to Mary Ellen but didn't let go when she put her hand on it.

"Actually, do you mind if I take a picture of it?" I caught her curious gaze and shrugged. "I don't know. Seems like it could be important."

"Certainly." She withdrew her hand, and I laid the receipt down on the counter. I pulled my phone out of my pocket and snapped a few pictures of the receipt, focusing on the signature at the bottom.

"Thank you," I said, slipping my phone back into my pocket. I turned to go and then turned right back around to Mary Ellen. "What did he look like?"

"He was nice looking. A little older than you. A little taller than me." She gestured a couple of inches above her head. She was tall, probably close to five foot ten, so I guessed the man was about six feet. "His hair was short. Dark. He had brown eyes and little wire-rim glasses." She curled her hands around her eyes to mimic glasses. "A beard." She rubbed her cheeks. "Just a short one. He wore a navy blue polo shirt and a pair of khakis. Very neat. Very well groomed. He seemed like a nice man." She shook her head. "It's a shame."

I nodded in agreement. "Thank you, Mary Ellen. For everything." I lifted the bag to indicate I meant both the food and the conversation.

"Come by any time. I enjoy your company."

I turned to go again then thought of another question before I made it out the door. If I were a detective, I would either be exceptionally bad at my job because I would only think of the most critical questions after I left, or I would be incredibly good at it because I would wear the suspects down, and they would confess just to keep me from coming back repeatedly with more questions.

"Mary Ellen?"

"Yes?"

"One more thing—did you give the police the man's name?"

Mary Ellen hesitated. "No, I didn't."

113

"Why not?"

"Well, they didn't ask."

I was surprised. I'd noticed Mary Ellen seemed reluctant to volunteer information to me, but I hadn't thought she'd be the same with the police. I wondered if she was hiding something.

"I was so shaken up when they were here, I didn't even think about the credit card receipt. I only thought of it late last night."

Well, at least that explained why she didn't tell the police—if she was telling the truth, that is.

"So, are you going to tell them?"

Mary Ellen smiled, apparently noticing my concern that she hadn't shared all the information with the police. "I called the officer this morning and left a message."

"Mike?"

"No, it was a young man. He interviewed me yesterday and left me his card. I can find it for you if you'd like."

"Was it Ryan? Leary?" I remembered the new-in-town officer Sammy and I had met the night before. "Tall, broad shoulders, dark hair, crew cut?"

"No, that wasn't him. Do you want me to find that business card?"

"No, it'll be all right. I was just curious. Thanks again."

I finally managed to leave Mary Ellen's then headed to the coffee shop. I snuck in the back door and peeked into the café. It was busy, but nothing Sammy and the girls couldn't handle.

Sammy looked up and caught my eye. I motioned that I was going to eat, and she nodded. Back in the stock room, I selected a tomato soup Mary Ellen had given me and heated it up in the microwave.

The soup was every bit as delicious as I expected. The broth was smooth and had the flavor of delicious, fresh, summer vine-ripened tomatoes. I probably could have eaten a gallon of it. Instead, I opened the box of marzipan and scanned through it, looking for which piece I wanted to indulge in.

I spotted a little tomato and smiled. What better dessert than a marzipan tomato after a lunch of tomato soup? I ate it and left the box open on the counter so Sammy and the girls could have some. I considered not sharing, but my grandfather's voice in my head reminded me to be kind to my employees.

I pulled an apron over my head, tied it behind my back, and went out front to the café.

"Where do you need me?" It was my café, but the girls had a good rhythm going, and I wasn't going to mess it up just because I was the boss.

Sammy looked around as she prepared a cappuccino. "Um, dishes? Or you can take over here after I finish this one, and I can wash dishes."

"Up to you." I much preferred to be behind the espresso machine, but I wasn't going to kick Sammy off if that's where she wanted to be.

She looked at me. "Nobody comes in here to see my latte art."

"Doesn't matter what the picture is if the coffee's bad. And you make good coffee."

"Yeah, but I'm not the one who earned a write-up in a food blog. Here." She stepped back from the machine, the cappuccino she'd been working on in a saucer in her hand. "I'll take this to the customer. You make the next one. Latte, double shot espresso. Gentleman in the corner, blue shirt."

I stepped up to the espresso machine, and Sammy walked around the counter to deliver the drink she'd just made. I checked the machine over quickly to make sure everything was ship-shape then started pulling the espresso shots.

While the machine worked, I began steaming the milk to pour into the cup. As I worked, I thought about the design I wanted to put into the latte's foam. I liked to start slow and not make anything too complicated until a few drinks in. I thought about a butterfly but decided on a star. Women tended to get more excited about butterflies and hearts, so I usually saved those designs for them.

The espresso and milk were ready. I leaned over the cup and began my pour. Once the dot of milk was in, I picked up the small metal etching tool and began drawing in the star. It only took a few seconds, and the star was beautiful when it was done. My grandfather would have been proud. It had always been his motto to "Make your food delicious, and make it beautiful." The delicious came first then the beautiful, but both were important.

I carried the cup and saucer to the blue-shirted man in the corner then returned to the espresso machine. There was no one else in line. The rush was over. I wiped down the machine and the counter.

Amanda was bussing the tables and taking the dirty dishes to Sammy in the back. Becky had started refilling the food in the display case without anyone requesting her to. I made a mental note to put a little something extra in her paycheck. Another thing I'd learned from my grandparents when they'd run the café was to reward people when you caught them going above and beyond.

I finished wiping everything down and went to help Sammy with the dishes. She had a stack of clean dishes that needed to be put away, so I worked on those.

"Sorry about your night out getting ruined last night," I said.

Sammy shrugged. "When you go out with Dawn, you have to expect things to go a way you didn't expect. It would have been more fun if it had turned into a spontaneous road trip to New York, though."

I didn't really think a trip to New York was as exciting as she did, only because I'd lived there for so long, but I had to agree it would have been preferable to checking out a crime scene. "Maybe we can try again next week. We'll be on fall hours then, so we'll have more time."

Like most businesses in Cape Bay, we basically ran three schedules—summer hours, spring/fall hours, and winter hours—depending on the expected amount of tourist traffic. With school starting the next week, we'd be closing earlier on the weekdays, finally giving us a chance to catch up on our personal lives.

"That sounds good. That mango margarita Dawn got right before we left sounded pretty good. I'd be up for going to get one."

"Tuesday night?"

"That'll be perfect!" She flashed me a sunny smile and seemed like her old self.

"What can I work on?" Becky stuck her head through the door. Her red curls were typically frizzy, the result of spending a morning over steaming cups of coffee. Amanda was hovering behind her also awaiting orders.

"How are we on sandwiches?" I asked.

"Good. Display case is fully stocked, and there are a few more in the refrigerator."

"What about tiramisu?"

"All filled up. Cupcakes and muffins are, too."

"There's some marzipan on the table over there," I offered.

"Where do you want me to put it?"

"No, for you. You and Amanda take some."

Becky approached the table cautiously and looked into the box. "What is it?"

"Marzipan." Then, I realized she had no idea what that was. "It's like candy."

"Oh, okay." She and Amanda peered at the figures in the box. "The animals are all too cute too eat." Becky picked up a heart instead.

Amanda and I both watched her face as she bit into it slowly. She looked very serious as she tasted it. Then she smiled. "It's good!" She pushed the box toward Amanda, who picked out a pine tree. Amanda smiled when the marzipan hit her tongue.

"Why don't you two each take a couple of pieces and go home for the day? Enjoy your last weekend before school starts. It's going to be dead in here the rest of the day anyway." Out of the corner of my eye, I saw Sammy make a face at my choice of words. The girls didn't seem to notice it, though.

"Awesome! Thanks!" They each picked out a few pieces and wrapped them in napkins. After they hung their aprons and fished their purses out of drawers, they waved goodbye and headed for home, or wherever else they spent their time when their parents thought they were at work.

Sammy and I went back to washing dishes. My mind returned to the man in the alley.

Chapter Nine

I spent the afternoon itching to get online to see if I could find information on an Abraham Casey, preferably one with short dark hair, dark eyes, a trim beard, and glasses. I was lucky the café was slow and I didn't have to concern myself too much with customers, although thinking about something else for a few minutes probably would have done me some good.

Half an hour or so before Sammy was due to leave, I ran home to let Latte out and play with him for a minute. When I got back, the café was just as empty as when I'd left, with just a couple of local moms lingering in some comfy armchairs, chatting quietly and enjoying the break from their kids. Having witnessed them come in before with their kids, I didn't blame them for wanting some time to themselves.

I greeted them with a wave and went in the back to put my apron on. I found Sammy slipping the last bite of a marzipan bunny into her mouth.

"Sorry," she mumbled around it. "I got hungry."

"With all the food in this café, you had to take my marzipan? I'm kidding—I left it there so you guys could eat it."

"That's what you said, but I know how you feel about marzipan."

I laughed. "And I thought I kept that so well hidden."

She smiled and slid her apron over her head. "Guess I better get going."

"Big plans tonight?" I hoped for her sake that she wasn't planning on spending the night at home on the couch with a pint of ice cream and a cry-your-eyes-out movie.

"I'm going over to help my mom with some canning while my dad watches college football and yells at the TV."

I thought that sounded less depressing than the movie and ice cream on the couch. "Well, have fun."

Sammy laughed. "I'll try. After a day spent over hot drinks and a hot dishwater and an evening spent over boiling water, sterilizing jars for preserves doesn't exactly sound like a great time, but I'll survive."

She slipped out the back door, and I looked around for something to occupy me until the café's traffic picked up again around dinnertime. That was when all the vacationers ventured out to see the town and when the locals who had been out running errands all day stopped in to pick up a quick sandwich or coffee to get them through the evening.

As usual, Sammy had left everything in immaculate condition. All the dishes—except the ones being used by the two women out front—were cleaned and put away, the display cases were fully stocked, and every last table and counter had been wiped down. I was grateful, of course, for her attention to detail, but it didn't leave me much to do to keep busy.

I let my hair down from its perpetual summertime chignon and ran my fingers through it. I noticed again how long it was and wished I had remembered to ask Sammy for a recommendation on a good place to get it cut. I'd have to remember to ask when I saw her tomorrow. I twisted my hair back up off my neck and secured it.

I was tempted to sit down at the computer and start researching the late Mr. Casey, but I restrained myself. My research could wait until I didn't have a business to run. Instead, I decided to roast a batch of coffee beans. It never hurt to have extra beans roasted. Unfortunately, roasting coffee beans didn't take much time or effort since the machine did most of the work, but it made me feel productive.

I stood and looked around the café. Mismatched chairs and tables lined the exposed brick walls. A few comfortable armchairs sat in the corner for people who liked to spend a little more time lingering over their drinks. A chalkboard menu, covered in Sammy's flawless handwriting and artful drawings, hung above the counter. It looked almost the same as it had when my grandparents were alive. It was warm and cozy and felt like home. I suspected it did for a lot of our customers, too, based on how often they came and how long they stayed.

The two women left, and I went into the back storeroom to organize. The bell over the door would let me know if someone came in. I managed to kill the rest of the afternoon until the evening rush started. I had a busy hour or so, but nothing I couldn't handle on my own. Of course, Chase Williams was in and out as I worked busily on making drinks. I waved hello, took his order, made his drink, and waved goodbye. I'd try to talk to him again next time.

I was grateful for the brief rush not only for the revenue and the fact that the increase in customers kept me busy for a while, but also because it stopped my attempts at organizing the storeroom. I'd managed to make the back room look messier than it had when I'd started. Sammy would have a fit when she saw it. Matt came in just as the rush subsided and saved me from doing any more damage.

"How's it going?" He walked up to the counter.

"Doing okay." I smiled. "Been pretty slow until the last hour or so." I shrugged. "But that's normal for a Saturday."

"You mind if I hang out for a while?" he asked.

"No. Why would I?"

"I was being polite."

"You're such a gentleman."

"A hungry gentleman, at the moment."

"And what can I get you, sir?" I asked in my politest café-owner voice.

"A latte, please." He leaned back to look into the display case. "And is that my favorite dark chocolate cupcake I see in there?"

"You know I make a point to always have it for you."

"The day I don't ask is the day you don't have it."

I slid open the door of the display case and pulled out one of the dark chocolate, peanut-butter-filled cupcakes he adored. I put it on a plate and handed it across the counter to him. "Go sit down. I'll bring your latte over in a minute."

Matt took the plate and settled at a table in the back corner. I turned to the espresso machine and started working on his coffee. The motions of preparing the drink were so familiar that I was reasonably sure I could do it in my sleep. I was glad because I needed to focus most of my mental faculties on deciding what design to put into the foam. I made Matt coffee so often that I always had trouble coming up with what to create.

I varied between the extremes of a simple rosette and the most complicated, creative, or quirky design I could think of. The time frame to decide was so short—only seconds from the time the espresso was ready until I had to start pouring—there wasn't really time to dwell on what I wanted to do. I smiled as the idea came to me and started pouring the milk.

There was no one else in line, so I quickly prepared a drink for myself and decorated it with a simple swan then carried both over to Matt's table.

"Mind if I join you?" I set the cups down. I made sure Matt's was angled just right so he could fully appreciate my hard work the instant he looked at it.

"Not at all," he said around a bite of cupcake. He gestured toward the chair on the opposite side of the table.

I sat down and waited while he chewed. He took so long that I started getting antsy. I was probably a little too excited about my design, but I thought it was really clever.

He finally looked down. He squinted his eyes a little, cocked his head, and smiled. "Latte?"

"Of course! That's what you ordered!" My lips twitched as I tried to keep a straight face.

"I didn't specify I wanted Latte in my latte."

"I figured I'd go literal." I smiled. I'd named my dog after the drink because they were the exact same color. It seemed only natural to recreate the dog in the drink.

"I gotta hand it to you, it looks exactly like him. I have no idea how you make something like this out of milk and coffee."

I resisted the urge to correct him and point out that a latte is made with espresso, not coffee. I had learned a long time ago the average person didn't care about the intricacies of the coffee world. I still had to bite my tongue to keep from correcting people, though.

Matt hesitated as he looked at the cup. "I hate to ruin it." He shook his head.

"There's no point if you don't drink it." I'd told him a hundred times before, and I'd probably have to say it a hundred times more. I loved how much he appreciated my creations, and I'd be a little disappointed the first time he didn't hesitate to ruin it.

Matt tipped the latte back and took a drink. "Delicious as usual."

I smiled with pride and took a drink from my own cup.

We sat peacefully for a few minutes, enjoying each other's company in silence. My mind cleared as I sat with Matt, and I didn't think about Abraham Casey for a change.

Finally, Matt spoke up. "Get the chance to talk to Mary Ellen today?"

"I did." I sipped my coffee. I felt a surge of excitement when I remembered what I had to tell him, but I held it in, or tried to.

"And?"

"He was in her shop right before he died."

"Buying souvenirs?"

"Buying souvenirs," I confirmed.

"So you were right."

"Yup, I was."

Matt looked at me, his eyes narrowed, and I fought back a smile.

"What else?"

"He paid with a credit card."

Matt thought for a minute. "So..." He paused. "He doesn't carry cash? He has a tough time at vending machines?"

"What's on a credit card?"

"A number. An expiration date. A verification number. Uh..."

I looked at him, wondering if he'd gone dumb or was just playing with me. "Really? Matty, come on. Under the number. Think about it, *Matteo Cardosi*." I emphasized the syllables of his name. "Are you really telling me, *Francesca Amaro*, that you can't think of anything else that might be on a credit card?"

I could practically see a light bulb turn on over his head. "A name!" And then he realized the significance of that. "You found out his name?"

"I did. Abraham Casey."

"Abraham Casey," Matt repeated. "Do you know anything else about him yet?"

"Yet? You just assume I'm going to keep investigating?"

Matt chuckled. "Well, I have met you."

Clearly, I was too predictable. "No, I haven't looked him up yet. I thought I should focus on running the café. Not that I'm doing a very good job of it right now." I motioned to a few tables scattered with dirty dishes. "I'll look him up later tonight."

"I'm impressed with your restraint." The corner of Matt's mouth twitched as he sipped his coffee.

I rolled my eyes, stood up, and downed the last of my latte. "But that reminds me— it's getting close to closing time. I should get to cleaning up."

"I guess I could help," Matt said, mock-reluctantly.

"You better get to it if you want to help me research one Abraham Casey later tonight."

"Oh, well, when you put it that way!"

Matt got up and helped me clear the tables, wipe everything down, and clean the dishes. By closing time, we had everything neat, clean, and ready to go for when Sammy opened up the next morning. The back room I'd turned into a chaotic mess would have to wait.

I locked up, and Matt and I started the walk home. We had gotten about halfway there when my stomach rumbled, and I realized I'd barely eaten all day.

"I need a lobster roll," I announced.

"Right now?"

"I've had a bowl of soup, some marzipan, and coffee today. I'm starving."

"Sandy's?"

"Yes." I turned on my heel and headed toward Sandy's Seafood Shack before Matt had a chance to react. After realizing I hadn't eaten, I seemed to get hungrier with every step.

"You really must be hungry." Matt hurried along beside me.

"I am." I paused. "Are you?"

"I could eat."

"That's not exactly convincing."

"I'm always up for lobster."

Sandy's was at the opposite end of the boardwalk, so it took us a little while to get there, but I wasn't complaining because I knew the warm, buttery lobster would be totally worth it.

When we got to Sandy's, we sat at one of the picnic tables on the back deck. Through the window screens, we could hear the ocean waves crashing. I took a deep breath of the tangy salt air. Since Cape Bay was a seaside town, the salt air was evident almost everywhere in town, but Sandy's deck literally hung out over the ocean, so the aroma was all encompassing. I loved it. It smelled like home.

We both ordered a lobster roll and a beer, as well as an order of fried clams to split between us. It was the best food I could imagine eating on a Saturday night in New England. Nothing compares to fresh-caught seafood.

Matt was in the restroom when the waitress brought the food to the table. I politely waited for him to return before digging into my lobster roll, but I went ahead and started popping the clams into my mouth. I told myself they were more like an appetizer than part of the actual meal, so it was okay to start without him.

"You gonna save some of those for me?" Matt asked as he returned to the table.

"If I have to." I was practically inhaling the crispy, delicious bits of clam.

He reached for one, and I swatted his hand.

"Do I have to fight you for them or something?"

"Or you could ask nicely." I shoved another piece into my mouth.

"May I please have some fried clams, Francesca, darling?" He batted the long lashes that encircled his warm brown eyes.

I took the clam that was almost in my mouth and put it in his outstretched hand. "You may have one."

Matt placed it delicately in his mouth then chewed very slowly.

I finally laughed. "Here, take them before I eat them all." I pushed the paper bowl toward him.

"I'll be fine if you just want to eat them."

"No, we got them to share."

"But if you're that hungry, I don't mind. I have plenty of lobster here. Unless you're planning to eat that, too."

"I'm not. I think I have enough on my own. But thanks for the offer." I lifted my lobster roll to my mouth and ate. It was perfection.

Despite my protests that I'd eaten more than half the food, Matt paid the bill when we finished, and we started the walk back to our street. Now that my stomach was full, the only thought on my mind was finding out just who Abraham Casey was.

Chapter Ten

Back at my house, we set up camp at opposite ends of the couch. Matt turned on a football game I couldn't have cared less about. I didn't even know they played football on Saturdays until he turned it on, although I did remember Sammy mentioning something about it earlier in the day.

When I asked Matt about the game, he launched into a lengthy explanation of the different types of football and their relative merits. I zoned out somewhere around "No, that's the NFL. This is college," which was almost immediately after he started talking.

Latte lay on Matt's lap because his hands were free for petting except when he used them to change the channel to a different game or for his beer-to-mouth weight-lifting exercises. Fortunately for Latte, Matt's intermittent activities only required one hand. My hands were occupied with my laptop. I was searching for Abraham Casey.

A surprising number of men had that name. I was glad his name wasn't John Smith or Mike Jones. I scrolled through the pages of search results, trying to figure out which one he might be. I ruled out the one who was born in 1783 and died in 1817 as well as his son and grandson. Several results just happened to have the words Abraham and Casey on the same page, including an article by someone named Casey Johnson about the biblical Abraham.

Another article featured an actress who played a character named Casey in a new movie, and someone with the last name Abraham had commented on it. I found it difficult to stay focused on my research because so many other things caught my attention.

"How's it going?" Matt asked when his game stopped for a studio-based segment with a bunch of brawny men and one busty blond woman wearing a dramatically low-cut shirt.

"Not great. I found a bunch of people named Abraham Casey, but I don't know how to narrow it down or figure out which one is the guy I'm looking for."

"Want me to help?"

"No." My stubbornness had kicked in, and I was determined not just to figure out who he was but to do it on my own. I felt as if I were so close, and if I just tried a little harder, there he would be. I tried my search again with Abraham Casey in quotes so it would only return results with both words next to each other.

"Any luck?" Matt asked later when another pretty blonde in a revealing top was interviewing a large sweaty man in football pads.

"No," I groused.

"Did you try social media?"

I shoved the laptop toward Matt. He perched it on the arm of the couch to keep from disrupting Latte.

"So what have you tried so far?"

I scooted next to him and listed off the things I'd tried. I'd been at it for so long, I knew I was probably forgetting half of it.

Matt clicked around and did a few general web searches then searched a couple of different social networks. I rested my chin on his shoulder as I watched him work.

"I can find a couple guys..." he murmured as he typed and clicked and scrolled and clicked and typed.

"A couple of guys?" I repeated when he didn't finish his sentence.

"A couple of guys who are at least sort of local. I figure they're the best ones to start with. There's one in Boston and one down in Hartford."

"You think either of them's him?"

"I don't know. The one in Boston's a pharmacist. The one in Hartford's a..." He scrolled and peered at the screen. "Mechanic."

"Mike and Mary Ellen both said the guy was dressed business casual. Can we check out the pharmacist first? Can we find out more about him?"

"Hold on one second." Matt typed in the search box again. He scrolled down the page and then back up. "You said Mary Ellen described him to you?"

I nodded without moving off his shoulder.

"Ouch! You have a pointy chin!" He pulled out from under my chin.

"Yes, she described him." I put my chin back where it was. He let me leave it there.

"What did he look like?"

"Brown hair, brown eyes, beard, glasses."

"That should narrow it down." I was reasonably sure he was being sarcastic, especially since brown hair and eyes described the majority of the world's population.

"Let me know if you see anyone who looks right." He pulled up a screen of people whose pictures were somehow associated online with the words "Abraham Casey." I was slightly embarrassed I hadn't thought to try that, but he didn't say anything, so I didn't either.

I looked at the screen. The first image looked as though it was from the article about Abraham in the Bible by Casey Johnson because it was an image of an old man with a long, flowing beard, a long cloak, and a shepherd's staff. The second picture was the actress who played Casey. The next few people were definitely not the man in the alley—too old, too young, too female. I let my eye wander down the page and gasped.

Matt saw it a second after I did. "This one?" He pointed at the image of a friendly-looking man staring out at us from the middle of the screen.

"Yup." The man had short brown hair, brown eyes, a trim beard, and glasses. He looked as though he were about five or ten years older than me.

Matt clicked on the picture, and we were taken to a social network we'd searched earlier to no avail. In the vast expanse of social media users, we hadn't been able to find the Abraham Casey we were looking for. But now he was smiling at us like he'd just been sitting there, waiting for us to show up. Above him on the screen was another picture of him. In this picture, a woman and child smiled beside him. His wife and son, I assumed.

"Wow," Matt said.

"What?"

Matt clicked around on the screen, flipping between tabs that showed a variety of information about the elusive Mr. Abraham Casey. His birthday with the year, his hometown, his current employer, previous employers, his wife's name, his son's name and birthdate, his friends, his interests, places he'd been—almost everything you could want to know about him.

"This guy is not concerned with privacy. Look." He clicked to the Friends tab. "No mutual friends. If we can see this, that means everyone can see it. Every detail of his life out here for anyone to see."

"Is that bad?"

Matt craned his neck to look at me since I was still leaning on his shoulder. "Are you serious?"

"Yes?"

"Oh, Franny." He navigated away from Abraham's page and clicked on a menu. He scrolled down, clicking more menus here and there. "Well, yours aren't as bad as his, but they could use some tightening up. Do you mind?" He hovered the mouse over one of the settings.

"Go right ahead. Fix me up. As long as I can still see the pictures of all my friends' vacations to exotic places, you can do whatever you want."

Matt clicked around for a couple of minutes. "There. Now you won't have strangers looking at your profile because they came across your name on the Internet somewhere and wanted to know everything about you."

"Thanks." Matt clicked back on Abraham's profile page. I noticed the little link to his wife's profile and pointed over his shoulder. "Can we go look at her page?"

Matt clicked on the blue text, and we were taken to her profile. It was empty except for a picture of her smiling next to Abraham and holding their son. It looked like it was from a professional shoot.

"At least someone in that family had some sense about privacy," Matt muttered.

"Can we go back to his page?" He clicked over, and I leaned in to get a better look at the screen. "Scroll down."

Abraham Casey's entire life was laid out in front of us in pictures and short lines of text. Romantic dinners he'd had with his wife. Vacations they'd taken with their son. Funny bumper stickers he'd seen while stuck in traffic. The annoying thing the woman in front of him in the grocery store line had done.

I was transfixed by the bits and pieces of a stranger's life. A stranger I still wasn't entirely sure was the man in the alley. I'd have to print out his picture and take it to Mary Ellen to see if she could confirm whether it was the man who had come into her store. Then something caught my eye as Matt scrolled down farther.

"Stop!" I put my hand on his arm. "Go back. Up. Up. There!" I looked at the screen in shock.

"Oh, Abraham," Matt whispered.

On the screen was a picture of Abraham Casey's driver's license with the caption, "Took 3 hours at the DMV, but I'm renewed!"

Along with his picture, his address, height, weight, and all the other information on a driver's license, Abraham's signature was at the bottom.

I looked around at the couch, the end table, the floor, and stuck my hand between the couch cushions.

"What are you doing?"

"Looking for my phone." I got up on my knees and felt my pocket. The hard rectangle was on the left. I pulled it out and unlocked it. I tapped furiously, trying to get to what I wanted.

"Now what are you doing?"

"Looking for something." I finally found it and held my phone up to the screen. The signature was the same on the driver's license and the credit card receipt.

"It really is him." Matt sounded vaguely surprised. To be honest, I was, too. A part of me hadn't thought we'd actually find him and that maybe Abraham Casey was a pseudonym, but there he was. If the name was a pseudonym, it was the one he used in his everyday life. This really was the Abraham Casey we were looking for.

I sank back down onto the couch. "Okay, even I wouldn't put my driver's license online like that."

Matt laughed. "Well, at least you know that much." We stared at the screen, stunned that we'd trapped our quarry. "Now what? Do we call Mike?"

I shook my head. "Mary Ellen already called the police."

"She did? Then what did we do all this searching for if the police already know his name?"

"I wanted to know who he was. Like, really. Who the man was and what got him killed."

"And did you find that?"

"I think I know who he was," I said slowly. "Or at least I will after I stay up half the night reading down through his page. But no, I don't know why he was killed."

"And you're sure now that he was murdered?"

"Mary Ellen heard him yelling 'no.' He was either murdered or wanted someone to think he was."

"Maybe he had a life insurance policy that doesn't pay out for suicide. He wanted to kill himself but wanted his wife and kid to get the money."

I thought about it for a few seconds. "I don't know. It still doesn't make sense to me. He bought a lot of stuff at Mary Ellen's. If he just wanted to get souvenirs to make it look good, why buy so much stuff? If he bought things he actually wanted his family to have, why risk them getting messed up or his family not getting them at all? I still think murder makes more sense. I just have to figure out why."

"Do you have any ideas?"

"Well, in New York, I would have said mugging gone wrong, but we don't really have a lot of muggings in Cape Bay, so that's probably out. Revenge? Vendetta?"

"Lovers' quarrel?" Matt suggested.

"You think Mrs. Casey—what was her name? Leah?—you think Leah killed him?"

"Or his lover. Or hers."

"Crime of passion. It's a possibility." I thought about it. If Leah had killed him, had she come to town with him? Or was he here to meet a lover and she'd caught them together? Or maybe Leah was the one in town for a tryst, and Abraham had interrupted them. But then why would he have bought souvenirs? What if it actually was random? A chill ran down my spine. A random murder was frightening to think about. "I need to find out why he was here and who he was with. That's what I need to know before I can figure out the rest."

Matt nodded and scrolled quickly to the top of Abraham's page. "Nothing since Tuesday." He scrolled down slowly, then faster, slowed down, sped up, and slowed down again. "And that seems unusual for him. It looks like he usually posts every day. Sometimes two or three times a day even."

"He only died last night, though."

"So something happened before that to make him stop posting."

"What's the last thing he put up?"

Matt scrolled up. Abraham had posted a picture of himself with his wife Leah and their son, sitting at what looked like a restaurant table.

"Dinner at Woodman's," I read off the screen.

"They look happy."

I leaned against the back of the couch. Why did he stop posting? What had he been doing that he couldn't—or didn't want to—post? I stared at the screen, thinking through the possibilities. I needed to find out what he had been doing in Cape Bay. He'd had dinner with his family in Boston on Tuesday and died in Cape Bay on Friday. I had to find out what happened between those days.

"So what are you thinking?" Matt asked.

"I'm going to find out why he was here."

"And how are you going to do that?"

"Well, we know he didn't spend a whole week here, so he probably wasn't staying in a rental house."

"So, the Surfside?"

"That's where I'll start."

The Surfside Inn was the biggest and most popular lodging place in Cape Bay, although that wasn't saying much. The inn had about twenty-five rooms, which was a lot compared with the next-largest places, a couple of six-room bed and breakfasts. In other words, it wasn't hard to be the biggest.

The inn was a nice enough place as far as I knew, although I'd never stayed there. I crossed my fingers that Abraham Casey had. I hoped the clerk remembered him and wasn't feeling shy. If I couldn't get any information, I would have to hit the ten or so bed and breakfasts in our town and the next.

But first, I was going to the Surfside Inn.

Chapter Eleven

Late the next morning, I stood outside the Surfside Inn. True to its name, it was located right on the beach and boasted that each of its rooms had an ocean view. I was pretty sure the majority of the rooms only had an ocean view if you leaned over the edge of the balcony and tilted your head a certain way.

The inn was a two-story, U-shaped building that looked as though it had been blue and white at some point but now was more grayish-blue and gray. All rooms opened to the exterior and shared a walkway that circled the building. A pool was located in the interior of the U, but that was on the ocean-facing side, and I was on the road-facing side. "Surfside Inn" was emblazoned across the marquee in large white letters with blue waves on either side. Predictably for Labor Day weekend, the "No" was lit up in the No Vacancy sign.

I took a deep breath, crossed my fingers, opened the front door, and walked inside. A bored-looking teenager slumped at the front desk, poking at his phone on the counter with one hand and resting his head in the other.

"Sorry, we're full," he muttered, not even looking up at me.

"I'm not looking for a room. I'm looking for a person."

He raised his eyebrows to look at me without having to change the angle of his head. I waited, but he didn't say anything.

"I think he's a guest of yours?"

He pointed with his cell phone-poking finger over at a phone in the corner. He managed to do it without changing his elbow's position on the table. It was quite a feat of stillness. "You can call his room from there. Just dial the room number." He went back to tapping at his phone.

I took a slow, deep breath through my clenched teeth. I stepped closer to the counter. "I don't know his room number. That's why I came in here."

"Oh. Well, can't you call his cell or something?" he asked without looking up.

Most of the time, I didn't feel much older than the teenagers I encountered, but this kid was making me feel every bit of our nearly twenty-year age difference.

I suddenly understood what my grandfather had felt when he called the more disrespectful teenagers he encountered "little twerps." This kid was a little twerp, and I was done with him. I placed my hands firmly on the counter and barely restrained myself from slamming them down as hard as I could. He finally looked fully up at me.

"Excuse me, young man, but I am asking you to please stop messing around on your phone long enough to help me with one simple request. Since that seems to be beyond what you are willing to do today, could you *please* go get your supervisor for me. And don't even try to tell me that you're the manager, because if you are, I want to see the owner. I have lived in this town long enough to be quite certain you are not that."

Before the little twerp could say anything, a middle-aged man came through a door behind him. He was balding slightly with a sizable paunch. Warm brown eyes shone out from behind the wire-frame glasses perched on his nose.

"Hi, I'm the owner. Can I help you?" he said kindly, stepping up to the counter. He completely ignored the little twerp, who leaned back in his chair and glared at me. I glared right back. He may not have known it yet, but I was winning this.

"Hi," I replied, just as nicely. The little twerp would see how customers and business representatives were supposed to interact. "I was wondering if you could help me with something. I'm looking for someone who I think might be a guest of yours." I cast a glance twerp-ward. "Would you mind if we spoke in private?"

"Of course. Come back around into my office here with me."

I stepped around the counter and went into his office. He gestured for me to take a chair and shut the door behind us. He sat down across the desk from me.

"Thank you for seeing me, Mr...."

"Martin. Edward Martin. And you, I believe, are Francesca Amaro."

"Yes, I am," I said, startled. "How—"

"You're Carmella's daughter."

I nodded.

"I've been too busy to make it over to Antonia's much this summer, but I usually make it up there quite a lot during the off-season. Your mother was a lovely woman. Her passing was quite a loss to the Cape Bay community."

"Thank you." His kind words made my throat tighten up.

"Of course, from everything I've heard, you're doing quite well yourself. A real honor to her memory. So, kudos."

"Thank you."

"Now, you said you're looking for a guest of mine?"

"Yes." I took a deep breath. I needed to get my mind off my mother and back on the case. "A Mr. Abraham Casey."

"Abraham Casey," he repeated. He turned in his chair toward his computer and punched a few buttons. After a moment, he nodded. "Yes, Room 205. But I don't think you asked to speak privately just to find out his room number."

I took a deep breath. I was worried about convincing him to give me information. I wasn't with the police, and I wasn't a friend or family member of Abraham Casey. I was barely an acquaintance of Edward Martin. He had no reason at all to give me the information I was looking for. To complicate matters, I didn't even know if the police had told him about the man's death. I certainly didn't want to be the one to break it to him.

"Is anyone staying here with him?"

"Just how do you know Mr. Casey, Francesca?"

"Fran, please. Call me Fran."

"And you can call me Ed." He paused, and I thought I was off the hook.

"How do you know Mr. Casey, Fran?"

I closed my eyes for a second and took a deep breath. I was at a crossroads. I could lie to this fellow local business owner, whom I would probably see around town on a regular basis, and risk any potential goodwill that might exist between us. Or I could tell the truth and risk not getting the information I was looking for. The little twerp out front certainly wasn't going to help me out. I needed to preserve my reputation in Cape Bay, but I needed the information, too.

I took a deep breath and opened my mouth, still not certain what was going to come out.

"I don't." I waited for him to kick me out.

"May I ask why you're inquiring after him?" he asked kindly.

There was something in the way he asked that made me willing to go out on a limb. "I think you may already know."

Ed leaned back in his chair and took off his glasses. He pinched the bridge of his nose and sighed. "I was afraid of that."

Afraid I was asking because I was nosing around a murder case? Or afraid Abraham Casey was the man in the alley everyone in Cape Bay had heard about?

"You're sure? That Casey is the dead man?"

"Reasonably so, yes."

"And you're asking about him because?"

"Because apparently it's what I do." I immediately realized how strange it must sound.

"Ah, yes, I'd heard about that." He slid his glasses back onto his face and leaned his elbows back on his desk.

Really? Everyone in town!

"It's nothing lurid, I promise. I'm not going to publish the information anywhere or anything. I just have questions. And if that gets people thinking and helps the police solve the case a little faster, then that's a good thing."

"It was a suicide, though, wasn't it?"

"It may have been." I stopped, wondering how much I should say. I didn't really know Ed, so as genial as he seemed, I decided it might be best to play some of my cards close to the vest. "Someone," I said, carefully omitting Mary Ellen's name, "heard shouting from the alley just before the gunshot. Maybe it was a suicide. But if it wasn't, it would be an injustice to let a murderer go free."

Ed nodded thoughtfully. He rubbed his hand over his balding head and sighed. "He was here alone," he said finally then made a face. "He checked in alone. One adult on the reservation."

I noticed the careful way he phrased it. "But?"

"The other night, uh, Thursday, I was here late taking care of a maintenance issue in 207—a clogged toilet—some college kid shoved a towel down in there and still thought it should flush. Dumb kids. Anyway, I was going out when Casey was coming in. I was the one who checked him in, so I knew he was alone. Except he wasn't alone." Ed paused and fidgeted uncomfortably in his chair. "He was with a young lady." He held up his hands quickly. "Now I'm not one to judge. A man can do whatever he wants with his time. In my hotel, as long as you're not breaking the law or disturbing the other guests, you're free to do what you please. Heck, for all I know, she was Mrs. Casey. He wore a wedding ring, you know."

I did know. I'd seen it in some of his many pictures online. And I'd also seen Mrs. Casey in some of those pictures. "Can you describe the woman he was with?"

"Are you sure you're not working for the police?" He chuckled.

"I'm sure." I smiled. "Just want to figure out who else I should talk to."

"Sure. She was young. A little older than the college girls who stay here a lot. Maybe in her mid-twenties, maybe a little older. She was a pretty girl. Blond hair, very tan.

She looked like she spends a fair bit of time on the beach. Her outfit didn't leave much to the imagination. She was very..." He cleared his throat and looked away from me. He lowered his voice to barely more than a whisper. "She was very well..." He paused again. "Very well endowed." He looked like he was beyond embarrassed. He paused, and I waited to give him time to get past his discomfort. "You know, come to think of it, I don't think she was his wife."

I choked back a laugh. The buxom blonde ten years or more his junior wasn't clean-cut, fastidious Abraham Casey's wife? No kidding! I supposed there had been more ridiculous pairings. Part of my disbelief likely had something to do with having seen pictures of the actual Mrs. Casey, who was beautiful in her own right, but much more of what you might expect the wife of a pharmacist from Boston to look like. Leah Casey was also blond but looked more the type to slather on sunscreen each day and wear sweater sets.

"What makes you think that?" I managed to ask and hoped I didn't give away how preposterous I found the very thought.

"Well, I just realized that I've seen her around town before. I think she's a waitress over at the Sand Bar."

Dawn bartended at the Sand Bar. If Ed was right, and Abraham Casey's mystery woman was a waitress there, Dawn might be able to tell me who she was. It was a lucky break.

"Was there anything else you noticed about her? Or him?"

Ed looked up toward the ceiling thoughtfully and drummed his fingers lightly on the desk. "No, no, not that I can think of. Is there anything you had in mind? Something in particular?"

"Did either of them say anything to you?"

"Not a word. Casey looked at me, but he didn't say anything. They both seemed pretty tipsy. She was hanging all over him, saying something about how she had been so stressed out and low on money and just needed to relax and was so glad she'd run into him. That was all I heard."

The interesting information certainly painted a different picture of the man than his social network postings.

"When he checked in, did he say why he was in Cape Bay?"

"He didn't. Most people come for vacation. I assumed he was here for that reason also."

"Did he have a reservation, or did he just show up?"

"Reservation." He punched a few buttons on his computer. "Made three months ago."

"For how long?"

He peered at the computer again. "Wednesday through Saturday."

"So not the whole weekend?"

"No."

"Is that normal?"

"Not at all. Wednesday through Saturday is a very unusual reservation span. We're not as structured as the houses, but for the most part, people stay a whole week, or Friday through Sunday, or sometimes just a night or two in the middle of the week. But Wednesday through Saturday, that's unusual."

I had asked every question I had come in planning to ask, but I took a moment to think. I wanted to make a smoother exit from the Seaside Inn than I had at Mary Ellen's the day before when I tried to leave three times before I finally ran out of questions. I didn't want Ed Martin's first impression of me to be that I was scatterbrained.

"What did you think of him? Abraham Casey, I mean," I asked finally. "What was he like?"

"He seemed like a nice man. Kind, friendly. Tried to offer me a tip just for checking him in. He didn't even need help with his bags. He kept his room very tidy but left generous tips for the maids each day. That's actually when I first suspected that it was him in the alley—Amelia mentioned that his bed hadn't been slept in and there was no tip. Now, don't get me wrong, it's not like they expect a tip each day. It's just that Casey had left a ten, clearly labeled as being for the maid, both of the previous nights. When nothing was disturbed Saturday morning, and there was no tip, but his bag was still there—well, I was concerned."

We sat for a moment and reflected on the dead man. Ed had met him personally and seemed to like him. I was just putting together a picture of him through his social media and the reflections of others. But both of us felt saddened by his passing.

"Well, I've certainly taken up enough of your time." I scooted to the edge of my chair. "Thank you, and it was a pleasure to meet you." I extended my hand across the desk, and he shook it.

"Thank you for coming by. You certainly jogged my memory. Do you think I should call the police to let them know that Casey was staying here?"

"They haven't been by yet?"

"No. I was holding out hope that it meant the man in the alley wasn't our guest."

I wondered if that was the case. Everything I'd found pointed in Abraham Casey's direction, and it would be an unbelievable coincidence if the dead man were someone else. "It can't hurt to call."

"You're right. I'll do that."

We stood, and he walked me to the door.

"Oh, one other thing." I nearly kicked myself for doing the exact same thing I'd done at Mary Ellen's. I stopped for a moment, trying to figure out how best to phrase what I wanted to say. "The young man at the desk—"

"My sister's kid." Ed cut me off. "I'd fire him if I could, but I'd get such a guilt trip about it from my mother. I just haven't worked up the nerve. I try to schedule him when there's not too much foot traffic in the lobby so I don't inflict him on too many people."

"I can't say I blame you for that." I bid Ed Martin farewell and went into the lobby. The little twerp didn't even glance up at me as I walked by. He made me glad I was an only child.

Chapter Twelve

On the way to the café, the weight of my thick hair reminded me to ask Sammy for a stylist recommendation. "Ask Sammy about hair. Ask Sammy about hair. Ask Sammy about hair. Ask Sammy about hair." I mentally repeated the phrase.

When I walked through the back door, Sammy was pushing the boxes I'd moved back to where they belonged on the shelves.

"Did you do this?" she asked immediately. She was very possessive of the storeroom organization. She considered it a personal point of pride that she knew where everything was and could produce it in seconds.

"Ask Sammy about hair," I said out loud.

"What?"

"Sorry, I've just been reminding myself. Yes, I did that. I'm sorry. I was trying to organize and—you know how when you try to clean up a room, sometimes it gets messier before it gets cleaner?" The look on Sammy's face indicated she was not familiar with that phenomenon. "Well, that's what happened. Also, can you recommend a good stylist? My hair is getting long, and I don't know who to go to."

"Everything was organized just fine before you went on your little..." She looked around as though baffled by what I'd done. "Your little rampage here. Don't do that again or at least tell me if you do. I can't find the napkins for the life of me. And Chase Williams down at Beach Waves. I've been going to him for years."

"Chase does hair? I had no idea." Why had no one ever mentioned my childhood neighbor had grown up to be a hair stylist? "And the napkins are over on the left side of the third shelf. P for paper."

Sammy looked at me blankly.

"I alphabetized everything. A through G is on the top shelf, H through N on the second, O through U on the third, and V through Z on the bottom."

Sammy blinked. She opened her mouth and closed it. She held up one finger. "Why not N for napkins?"

"I thought all the paper products should be together."

"And alphabetized under P."

"Uh-huh."

Sammy looked at me, and from her expression, I couldn't tell if she wanted to hug me, pat me on the head, or cry. "Please do not organize."

I laughed. "That bad, huh?"

"Yes. That bad."

"I thought it kind of worked."

"Oh, Fran."

"No?"

"How many supplies do you think we have that can be categorized as V through Z?"

"Water?"

"We get that from a tap," she whispered, sounding somewhat exasperated.

"Good point."

"Please don't organize again." I was now certain she wanted to pat me on the head.

"Yes, ma'am."

"You better be glad I love you." She gave me a hug then looked at my face and shook her head.

"You better be glad you're great at your job. You couldn't get away with talking to your boss like that just everywhere, you know," I teased.

"Is that a threat?" she joked back.

"No, the café would go under without you. It was just a statement of fact."

Sammy laughed. "Come over here and help me put everything back where it belongs."

I tilted my head to see how Becky was doing out in front. It wasn't very busy, and she looked as though she had everything under control. "Do you think Becky's doing okay? I could go out there and help her," I said just to irk Sammy.

"No!" She laughed. "You will stay here and fix what you messed up, young lady!" I hadn't seen her in such a good mood in weeks, and I wondered if the time spent canning with her mother had done her good or if it was something else.

"Yes, Sammy." I gave in to my fate of straightening up. I let Sammy direct me for the most part, and as we worked, we actually came up with a better organizational system. I made a mental note to point out that my messing with things had turned out for the best after all. But at the moment, I had something else I wanted to bring up.

"Hey, do you know if Dawn is working tonight?"

"I think so. Labor Day weekend. People will want to go out and party more than usual for a Sunday because of the holiday tomorrow. Why?"

"I just wanted to ask her about something. I figured I may as well try to catch her at work."

"You want to talk to Dawn about something?" She knew full well Dawn and I really only socialized because of her.

"Yeeaah." I drew the word out. I hadn't told Sammy about my investigation into Abraham Casey's death, although I knew she probably wouldn't be surprised based on my recent track record.

Sammy studied me like a parent looking for signs of a lie in her child's face. "Are you investigating again?"

"It just didn't make sense to me that it was a suicide. I started looking into it, and the man was seen with a girl who may work at the Sand Bar. I thought Dawn might know her."

"You've figured all that out in a day and a half? While still working here, and I'm going to guess sleeping once in a while?"

I nodded.

"Have you ever thought about giving up coffee and joining the police force?"

"Do you really think Mike would let them hire me?"

"Good point." We moved boxes for a few more minutes before Sammy thought of something. "Oh, if you want to get Chase to cut your hair, you should probably go ahead and call over there. He books up really fast. It may be a while before he can get you in. He's really good, though. It's worth the wait."

I grimaced like a pouty child who didn't want to wait, but in the interest of getting my hair done as soon as possible, I called the salon.

"Good news!" I said to Sammy when I got off the phone a few minutes later. "He had a cancellation for Tuesday morning and got me in!"

"Must be your lucky day!"

It certainly seemed like a good day so far. I'd gotten a great lead from Ed Martin on Abraham Casey, and I'd gotten an appointment in less than forty-eight hours with my old neighbor who was now apparently the top hair stylist in the bustling metropolis of Cape Bay. I only hoped my luck held out, and I would be able to find out from Dawn the identity of the woman Abraham Casey had taken to his hotel room.

I didn't have much time to dwell on my luck the rest of the afternoon. The café got busier than I'd seen it on a Sunday afternoon. Predictably, Chase Williams breezed in and out during the busiest time. I began to wonder if he somehow did it on purpose. Maybe he wanted coffee but didn't want to talk to me. If that were the case, he could just come when I wasn't there. Of course, for all I knew, he did.

The rush lasted an exceptionally long time, and both Sammy and Becky ended up staying long past the time they were supposed to leave. Everything finally calmed down near closing time, and I managed to shoo them out.

"Take tomorrow off!" I joked as they left. Antonia's, like every other locally owned business in Cape Bay, would be closed for Labor Day. We closed for most holidays—Easter, Memorial Day, Fourth of July, Labor Day, Columbus Day, Thanksgiving, and Christmas at a minimum. We had never decided to open those days when so many other businesses across the country had. It was a point of pride for us that we cared more about our workers and our community than the added revenue we would earn from opening on holidays.

Matt came in just as Sammy and Becky left. He put his hand on my waist and kissed me lightly. "How'd your day go?"

"Busy! I don't know where all those people came from. It was like every single person in town for the weekend suddenly felt compelled to get some coffee. Did you get over to my house to take care of Latte?" Partway through the afternoon when I realized I wouldn't be able to get away long enough to run home, I'd texted Matt and asked him to feed Latte and let him out.

"You know I did. We had a good time. Took a walk and everything."

"You're a good boyfriend." I stood on my tiptoes to kiss him on the cheek. He wasn't much taller than me, but it was enough that I had to make an effort.

"You know it. What about your trip to the Seaside?"

It took a second to realize he was referring to the motel, not the oceanfront. One of the downfalls of living in a beach town was half the businesses had a beach theme in their name—Seaside Inn, Sand Bar, Sandy's Seafood Shack, Beach Waves. It was as if we just couldn't stop ourselves.

"Better than I expected," I said after I figured out what he meant.

"Yeah? He was staying there?"

"More than that." I filled him in on everything I had found out in my meeting with Ed Martin.

"So I take it we're going out drinking tonight?" he asked after I told him I wanted to ask Dawn about the blonde Ed saw at the motel.

"You can drink. I have interviews to do."

"You're so professional," he teased.

I didn't have much left to do before closing the café. We had gone from incredibly busy to completely empty—a usual occurrence for the café. Sammy had refused to leave until everything was completely in order—as much as it could be, considering we were still open. Becky wouldn't be outdone and stayed right along with her. When closing time officially rolled around, Matt helped me shut the machines down and stow the food away. I grabbed the box of marzipan from the table in the back. I had found myself craving the sweet treats the night before and thought it would be prudent to bring them home with me to snack on during my much-anticipated day off.

"You want to run home to change?" Matt asked as we left the café.

"What? You don't like my stylin' work clothes?" I gestured to my outfit and struck what I considered a vaguely modelesque pose.

"They're fine. I just thought you might want to get changed before we went out."

"It's not really 'going out,' is it? I mean, I'm just going over there to ask Dawn who that girl is."

"Up to you." Matt shrugged.

We walked along a little farther before I abruptly turned down a side street.

"Where are you going?" Matt hurried after me.

"I decided you were right. We're going out. I can put on something that doesn't have coffee stains on it. Besides," I said, holding out the box of marzipan. "If I carry this into the bar, I might have to share it. Can't have that."

"Bar-goers are known for how much they enjoy a nice piece of marzipan with their tequila shots," he deadpanned.

I greeted Latte as I hurried into the house then left him to play with Matt while I ran upstairs to change. I didn't have time to take a shower as I would have liked before a date, but I changed into a cute pair of jeans and a nice top before touching up my makeup.

I let my hair down but didn't like the way it looked and tied it right back up again. I declared my reflection in the mirror more than satisfactory and headed downstairs to Matt and our date at the Sand Bar.

Chapter Thirteen

"Wow."

"What?"

"You look nice." Matt smiled.

"Thanks!" I was glad I had put extra time into my makeup and kind of wished I'd left my hair down. I knew it wouldn't have lasted, though, and I would have put it back up almost as soon as we walked out the front door. "You look...the same as you did when I went upstairs." We both laughed. "Handsome, though. I don't think I told you that earlier."

"Thank you."

I bent down to scratch Latte's head. "You be a good boy while I'm gone, okay? Did Matty give you a treat? Do you have a chewy?" I looked to Matt for answers since Latte wasn't exactly the most forthcoming with information.

He shook his head. "I didn't give him anything."

"Well, somebody needs a treat then, doesn't he?" Even as the words came out of my mouth, I couldn't believe I was baby-talking Latte in front of Matt. But it was probably a good sign for our relationship that I felt so comfortable with him.

I got Latte a treat and a rawhide from the kitchen. We went through his commands—sit, speak, lie down, roll over—and I rewarded him with his treat. Just before Matt and I walked out the door, I gave Latte the rawhide. "Now, you be a good boy while Mommy's gone! I love you!"

"You spoil that dog," Matt muttered as we walked toward the street.

"Oh, and you don't?"

"You're around him more than I am. My spoiling is like a favorite uncle. Yours is like, I don't know, an overly indulgent mother. Sorry, not a very good analogy."

"I don't think that was an analogy at all."

"I'm an engineer, not an English teacher."

We walked along Cape Bay's dimly lit streets, bantering back and forth about whatever mundane thoughts sprang into our minds. I felt remarkably safer with Matt than I had just two nights before when I had walked this path on my own. And then, I'd thought the man in the alley had killed himself. Now, I was reasonably sure he'd been murdered. By most measures, I should be much more nervous walking around now that I knew there was a murderer on the loose, but I also knew Matt would do whatever he had to do to keep me safe, and that made all the difference in the world.

We got to the Sand Bar in about ten minutes. While most of Cape Bay was deserted—there were barely any cars out driving around, and every business that wasn't a restaurant was closed—the Sand Bar was packed. The parking lot was full, and cars lined the street for at least a block in each direction.

"Is it always like this?" I asked.

Matt shrugged. He wasn't the barfly type.

We walked into the bar past the crowd spilling out the front door. It smelled like stale beer and hot, sweaty people. A band was set up on the stage, playing so loudly I couldn't even tell what the song was. I could feel the beat in my chest and thought if I tried hard enough, I might be able to pick out the song just based on that.

I hated when bands turned their amplifiers way up when they played in a relatively small place, like in restaurants, where you had to scream at the server just to give your order. Amps needed to be turned down lower in those situations. I sometimes wondered if bands kept them loud because they'd ruined their hearing over the years and honestly thought they were playing at a reasonable volume.

Once in a while, we had musicians play at Antonia's, and our long-time policy was that those musicians would play acoustic. It had started back in my grandparents' time when their friends would come in, sing, and strum the same guitar they played for their children at home. Electric guitars weren't as popular then as they'd become over the years, so it may have been that, also. Pianists were the one exception to the rule. We obviously didn't have a piano in the café, so piano players had to bring a keyboard, which they were allowed to plug in. It's hard to hear the melody from an unplugged keyboard.

"Why are they so loud!" I screamed in Matt's ear, the volume of my voice so high that it was impossible to make it actually sound like a question.

"So you can't tell how bad they are!" he yelled back.

That seemed like a distinct possibility, and I wasn't exactly going to give them a ringing endorsement based on the ringing I'd have in my ears long after their performance ended.

"You want to get a table!" Matt hollered.

I nodded, grateful that yes and no could be communicated without actual speech. He took my hand and led me through the maze of tables to a high-top table on the far wall.

"How's this!" he shouted.

I nodded again.

"I'll go get our drinks!"

I shook my head.

He crinkled his forehead and leaned his ear in to my mouth.

"I need to talk to Dawn!"

He shook his head, still not understanding.

"She's the bartender!"

He turned his head so that his mouth was next to my ear.

"Is she here?"

I stood on my tiptoes, balancing myself with a hand on Matt's shoulder, and craned my neck toward the bar. I could see Dawn darting between the shapes of people sitting on barstools. I pulled Matt down toward me. "Yes!"

"Are you going to be able to hear her over all this!"

He had a point.

I opened my mouth to bellow that I didn't know, when the band's noise came to a crescendo so loud I couldn't possibly yell over it. The guitar player wailed on his instrument. The drummer seemed to have his sticks on every single drum at once. And then it all stopped.

"We're going to take a break, but don't go anywhere 'cause we'll be right back!" the lead singer shouted into the microphone. I wondered if he understood how micro-phones worked.

"Depends on whether or not her hearing has been permanently damaged by all the noise yet," I said in what I hoped was a normal tone of voice. I could only hear the reverberations of my voice through my skull, so I couldn't actually be sure if I was whispering or screaming.

"Get me a beer?"

"Sure thing." I hurried away before he could realize that if I was ordering the drinks, I was the one paying for them. Who paid when we went out was a long-standing battle between us—each of us vying to treat the other. We once talked about each paying our own way, but the first time we went out with that intention, we both tried to slip the waitress our credit card within the span of roughly two minutes. We went right back to openly competing.

I wedged in between two tough-looking guys who had stationed themselves at the bar and tried to catch Dawn's eye. She was working the side of the bar I was on, and a rather nice-looking guy was working the other side. He wore a tight white T-shirt and tight black jeans. Dawn wore a deep scoop-neck tank top and a tiny pair of shorts.

I wondered if she got so hot working behind the bar that she had to wear skimpy clothes to keep cool. Then I saw the way the guys at the other end of the bar waved her over even though the other bartender was closer, and I realized her outfit was probably more to improve her tips than her comfort. When the other bartender came down to take my order, I realized the system worked both ways.

"What can I get you?" He put an elbow down on the bar, which I suspected he did mostly to give himself the opportunity to flex his bicep.

"Her." I pointed at Dawn.

He looked surprised. "Oh, all right."

"She's a friend," I said hurriedly.

He shrugged his muscular shoulders. "Dawn!"

She turned around, and he pointed his thumb over his shoulder at me. I smiled at her and waved. She rolled her eyes when she spotted me but moved toward me. Muscles made his way back to the other end, where there was a shortage of girls but plenty of thirsty guys.

"What do you want?" Dawn made a face as though she thought I wasn't cool enough to be at a bar.

I almost gave her a line about how she owed me a drink to make up for my ruined girls' night out but decided it wouldn't help my case. I needed her to want to talk to me. "I need to ask you about something."

She looked up and down the bar at the mass of people that had gathered. Apparently, I wasn't the only one who thought the band's break was the best time to get the bartender to hear you. "Can it wait? I kinda got a full crowd right now."

"Sure." I hoped she wasn't going to make me wait until after the bar closed.

"When the band comes back on."

She must have seen the concern in my face as I wondered how on earth we'd hear each other. "We'll go in the back."

I agreed.

"That it? You gonna order a drink, or are you just taking up my tip-earning time?"

"A beer. And can you make a margarita?"

She rolled her eyes. "Regular, on the rocks only. Frozen takes too long."

"That's fine."

She stared at me, waiting for I didn't know what.

"What?" I asked finally.

"What kind of beer?"

"Oh, um, I don't know. It's for Matt. Whatever you think he'd like."

She rolled her eyes again. I thought about saying what my grandmother would have—if she didn't stop rolling her eyes, they'd get stuck like that—but I thought wiser of it. She walked away. I waited, cash in hand, for her to come back, then handed her my money and told her to keep the change.

"Thanks." She looked less than impressed. I wondered if I should have tipped her more or if she would have reacted the same no matter what I gave her. I decided it didn't matter and went back to find Matt.

"Find out what you wanted to know?" he asked as I set his beer down in front of him.

"She told me to come back when the band starts back up."

"She really doesn't want to talk to you, does she?"

"I don't think so, but she said we'd go in the back."

Matt tasted his beer. "This is good. What is it?"

"I don't know." I shrugged. "I told Dawn to just give me something she thought you'd like."

"No wonder she doesn't want to talk to you."

I sipped my margarita, slightly afraid she might have poisoned it, but it turned out to be really good. Maybe Sammy wasn't the only reason she tolerated me after all.

After only a few minutes of relative quiet, the band reappeared on stage.

"Are you ready for some music!" the lead singer screamed into the microphone. He really didn't know how they worked. "Let's go!" The band struck their first note, and I resisted the urge to cover my ears.

Matt pointed past me toward the bar, and I turned to see Dawn beckoning me to follow her. I waved to Matt because it wasn't worth destroying my voice to tell him what he already knew then picked up my margarita. It was too good to leave behind on the table to get watered down as the ice melted.

Dawn pulled keys out of her tiny shorts and used them to unlock a door that was labeled "Employees Only."

"We had to start locking it because the drunks kept coming in and crashing on the couch." She closed the door behind us. The noise from the bar was suddenly deadened. "Sound proofing," she said when she saw my surprised look. "So what's up?" She flopped down on the couch.

"This is really good." I indicated the margarita. "And Matt liked his beer, too."

"That's what you wanted to talk to me about? You just knew you'd want to thank me for a drink you hadn't even ordered yet?"

"I was being nice."

"Sorry. Thanks. I actually kind of like it sometimes when people ask me just to get them whatever. Gives me a chance to get creative."

"You're good at it."

"Thanks. So what did you want to talk about?"

"Well, I've, uh, I've been kind of looking into that suicide the other night."

Dawn laughed her biggest, fullest, Dawn-est laugh. "Oh, I love it. Mike tells you to stay out of it, and the first thing you do is go poking your nose into things. You know, I think you're cooler than you act, Fran."

"Thank you?" I wasn't sure if I was supposed to take that as a compliment.

"It's a good thing." She answered my unspoken question. "But I'm guessing you're not here just to fill me in on that fact."

"Well, no." I sat down on a chair opposite her. "First thing, I don't think it was a suicide."

"There wouldn't really be anything for you to investigate if it was, would there?"

"Not really. The reason I'm here, though, is that I found out who the guy was and talked to somebody who saw him with a girl the other night."

"Wasn't me," she said immediately.

"No, I know it wasn't you. But I think she might work here."

Dawn raised her eyebrows but didn't say anything.

"Mid to late twenties, blond, really tan, busty. Dresses kind of provocatively. Well, at least when she's going back to a guy's hotel room. The person I talked to said he thinks she's a waitress here."

"Who'd you talk to? Eh, it doesn't matter," she said when I hesitated.

I took a sip of my margarita and swallowed hard. "So, do you know who she is?"

Dawn narrowed her eyes at me and pursed her lips. "Yup."

Chapter Fourteen

"You do?" I couldn't believe Dawn would be able to identify the girl I was looking for based on a description that probably fit fifty different girls in Cape Bay.

Dawn nodded. "You think she killed him?"

I opened my mouth to say no then reconsidered. "Maybe. I don't know her. Do you think she could kill a man?"

Dawn thought for a minute. "Depends on what he did to her."

I let that sink in. I hadn't put much thought into why Abraham Casey was murdered, just who he was and why he was in town. I still wanted to know why he was in town, but now that I was talking to people who had interacted with him, I needed to be on the lookout for potential suspects. And potential motives. If Abraham Casey had taken a girl up to his hotel room, maybe under duress, coercion, or something worse, she might have a motive. But I wouldn't know until I talked to her.

"I need to talk to her, Dawn."

She stared at me for so long that I was sure she was going to say no. Then she sighed. "Her name's Suzy. Suzy Frazier."

"Is she here tonight?"

Dawn nodded. "I'll point her out to you."

"Could you introduce her to me?"

"You're pushing your luck."

"Sorry."

"Oh, come on. Of course I'm going to introduce you to her. You're going to tell her I told you who she was anyway, right? I may as well be there to make sure she knows you're not some stark raving lunatic or the dead guy's wife or something."

"Thank you."

She shook her head and rolled her eyes again. I watched in hopes they would stick, but they didn't. They went right back to their normal place in her head.

"You ready?"

"To talk to her?"

"No, to go to the mall. Of course to talk to her." It was painfully obvious that even if Dawn was willing to defend me against a potential suggestion that I was a lunatic, she was completely convinced I was the dumbest person she'd ever met. But for some reason, probably Sammy, she was nice to me.

"Yes, I'm ready."

Dawn reluctantly got up and walked to the door. With her hand on the doorknob, she turned and looked at me. "Get ready." She opened the door, and the screaming music blared into the room. It was so much worse than I remembered. She gestured for me to follow her, and we made our way across the barroom floor. I waved and smiled at Matt as we passed. He tipped his beer glass at me.

Dawn walked up to a girl who fit Ed Martin's description of the woman he'd seen almost exactly. The only thing I would have added was that she wore a lot of makeup. But I expected he hadn't been paying that much attention to her face.

Dawn put her mouth to Suzy's ear and gestured at me. Suzy looked at me and nodded a couple of times, listened again, and nodded some more. I couldn't imagine what Dawn was saying except maybe, "Take pity on her. She's stupid, but she's my best friend's boss." As long as Suzy talked to me, I didn't care what Dawn told her.

Finally, they walked back in my direction. Dawn breezed by me, but Suzy came up to me and assumed the now-familiar mouth-to-ear position.

"You want to go outside?" she bellowed into my ear.

I nodded and followed her outside, pausing to drop my now-empty margarita glass at the bar as I went. She walked a short distance past the people gathered outside the door, most of whom had cigarettes between their fingers or dangling from their lips. Once we were out of earshot, Suzy stopped and leaned against the building. She pulled a pack of cigarettes and a lighter out of her pocket. "Want one?" She held a cigarette out to me.

"No thanks." My voice sounded very strange in the relative quiet of the outdoors after all the noise inside the bar.

Suzy put the cigarette in her mouth and lit it, taking a long draw. "So, Dawn said you want to talk to me?"

"Yeah, if you have a minute."

"I got about ten." She held out her cigarette and nodded at it.

"I'm Fran." I figured my name was a reasonable place to start.

"Suzy."

"Hi Suzy." I smiled.

"What is this? AA?"

"Sorry," I muttered. I felt like we were already getting off on the wrong foot. I took a deep breath. "Look, let me cut to the chase. I heard you might have gone back to a guy's hotel room with him Thursday night."

"So what if I did? You his wife or something?"

"Dawn said she was going to tell you that I'm not."

"She did. She said you're a friend of hers."

"She did?" I was shocked Dawn had called me a friend.

"Yeah, aren't you?"

"Yeah, I guess so."

Suzy gave me her version of the look Dawn liked to give me—the "are you stupid?" look. "You guess so? You don't know who your friends are?"

"No, I do, it's just that Dawn-I-well, never mind. We're friends. I'm not the guy's wife. I just want to know if you're the girl who went up to his room, and, if you are, maybe you could answer a few questions for me."

"You police?"

"No."

"Then why you asking questions?"

"Curious, I guess."

"About whose hotel room I'm going to."

"No, I'm curious about the guy. He—you know the guy they found in the alley the other day?"

"Yeah?" Of course she did. Everybody did.

"I think that was him. The same guy. The guy whose hotel room you went to, I mean. If that was you." We were back on the wrong foot, and I was struggling to get things back on track. It seemed as though her cigarette was disappearing into thin air right before my eyes. Which I guess, in a way, it was.

"Hmph." I couldn't tell if she didn't care, wasn't surprised, or was glad he was dead. Two of the three possibilities interested me. One concerned me.

"So, it was you?"

"Yeah, it was me."

"Did you happen to know his name?"

"What are you trying to say?"

I realized how my question must have sounded. "No, I just mean—I want to make sure it was the same guy. And I'm curious as to whether he gave you his real name."

She looked at me through narrowed eyes as she took a long drag from her cigarette. "It was the same guy."

My heart thudded. What was she saying? "How do you know?"

"You wouldn't be here if it wasn't. You didn't find me by accident."

I wasn't sure if her answer made me more or less suspicious of her. I tried to refocus her on my questions, and I was now uneasy enough that I knew I needed to pay close attention to her reactions. "What did he tell you his name was?"

"Abe. He didn't offer a last name, and I didn't ask. Wasn't like I told him mine either."

Abe. I wondered if that was what he went by all the time, what his wife called him. "Did you know he was married?"

She shrugged. "Didn't care."

"How did you meet him?"

"Here. He came in looking for a buzz and a good time. I was waiting on him. He was flirting pretty hard. Stayed around until closing time and asked me what I was up to after. I didn't have any plans, so I went back to his room with him."

"And did you–" I started to ask, then stopped. "Never mind, I don't want to know."

Suzy looked at me out of the corner of her eye and smirked. I got the feeling she thought I was as much of an uptight prude as Dawn thought I was a dumb bore.

"I mean...just never mind." I took a deep breath. "What was he like?"

Now Suzy smiled for real. "He was real nice. Real friendly. A charmer. Knew how to make a girl feel good about herself. And he threw around money like it was nothing."

"Really?" I was surprised even though her statement was consistent with what Ed Martin had said about Abraham Casey's tipping habits.

"Yeah, only wanted the top-shelf stuff, bought a round for the whole bar, gave me a tip that was more than I usually make in a whole night. Nice guy. Real shame."

The way she spoke, I couldn't tell if she honestly thought his death was a real shame, or if she meant it the way movie mob bosses said "it would be a real shame if something happened to that nice new car of yours."

"Did he tell you anything about himself? About his family?"

"What, do you think we sat around and talked all night?" She rolled her eyes.

I wondered if eye rolling was something the bar taught in its new-employee orientation. I decided it was more likely part of the interview process.

"No, he didn't talk about his family or anything. I knew he was like a pharmacist or something because he—" She paused and cast a sideways glance at me. "Because he mentioned it. And he didn't have to tell me he was from Boston because I could hear it when he talked. Southie, I think. Could be wrong about that, though."

Her cigarette was almost gone, and I searched my mind frantically for other important questions to ask. I got the feeling there would be no doorknob questions—no turning around at the last second to ask one more thing. When Suzy Frazier was done with her cigarette, she was going to be done with me.

"Did he mention anyone who might have wanted to kill him?"

"You mean other than himself?"

"He told you he wanted to kill himself?" If that were true, then the whole murder theory might be dead in the water. A man who said he wanted to kill himself and then died, apparently by his own hand, looked an awful lot like a suicide, no matter how many souvenirs he bought just before his death.

"No, but he did, didn't he? Kill himself?"

"I think it was murder."

"Oh, you do, do you now? And what makes you think that?"

"He bought a bunch of souvenirs just before he died. A big bag of them. Stuff for his wife and kid. Why would a man buy presents for his family and kill himself right after?"

Suzy seemed to go pale, though it was hard to tell from the dim parking lot lights. "He didn't say anything about anyone wanting to kill him. Until just right now, I didn't hear anything about anything but suicide, okay? I can't help you with that."

"Okay, okay, I'm sorry. I didn't mean to upset you."

"I ain't upset."

"I'm—I'm sorry," I said again. "Can you just tell me one last thing?" I asked as she dropped her cigarette and ground it out with the toe of her worn boot.

"What?"

"Did he tell you why he was in town?"

She stared at me, and I could see her tongue working around in her mouth. She was either debating with herself whether she wanted to tell me something or trying to get something out of her teeth. "No. He didn't say. Like I said, we didn't talk much."

I decided to make one last effort. "Is there anything else I should know about him?"

She stared at me again for an uncomfortably long period of time. Finally, she closed her eyes and sighed. She shook her head. "He could help you relax. If that was something you needed. And that's it. That's all I got to say to you. I got to get back to work." She brushed past me and headed for the door.

I stared after her for a second, not sure what had happened or what she meant. She had taken offense at almost everything I had said and seemed to be lying or hiding something in her responses. I didn't know if there was actually something to it or if she just didn't like me.

Slowly, I walked back into the bar. The music was louder and worse than I remembered. I wound my way through the tables to Matt. He was halfway through what I guessed was his second beer based on the fresh margarita sitting across from him.

I hopped into my seat and took a sip of the drink. It was as delicious as the first one. "Thank you," I mouthed to him, lacking the energy to scream after my conversation with Suzy. He pointed past me in the direction of the bar.

I turned around and saw Dawn looking at me. She raised her eyebrows and gave a thumbs up. Understanding that she was asking how the drink was, I smiled and gave her a thumbs up in response. Maybe she knew I would need another drink after talking to Suzy, or maybe we really were friends.

Matt and I finished our drinks without trying to talk. When we were done, he pointed toward the door, and I nodded. We slid off our chairs then made our way through the bar with me in the lead and Matt following with his hand gently brushing the small of my back. When we got outside, he took my hand.

"How did that go?" he asked loudly.

"I don't think you have to talk that loud," I said at what I thought was an appropriate volume.

"What?" he asked, even louder this time.

"Shh!" I whisper-shouted. I pulled him down toward me. "You're going to wake up the whole town," I said into his ear.

"Sorry." He spoke more quietly this time, but still on the loud side. "How did it go?"

I gave him the highlights of my chat with Suzy in as loud a voice as I dared. He nodded at appropriate parts, giving me the impression he understood at least most of what I was saying.

"There's something more to the story she's not telling you." His voice was a much more appropriate volume now. I was glad, not just because I didn't want him waking up the neighbors but also because I had been starting to worry about long-term hearing damage.

I agreed with him. "I just wish I knew what it was. Or at least whether it's important or not. I mean, it could be anything from she stole twenty dollars from him to she killed him. I just don't know."

"Add that to your list of things you have to figure out."

That list was getting pretty long.

Chapter Fifteen

As I lay in bed that night with Latte by my side, I was unable to fall asleep for the life of me. I just couldn't get the information I'd learned about Abraham—Abe, according to Suzy—out of my head. I'd started the day with my perception of him completely shaped by his social media profile—an outgoing, open, gregarious type of guy, a clean-cut family man. Now that I'd talked to a couple of people who had actually interacted with him while he was in Cape Bay, I was getting a completely different perspective of him.

He still seemed outgoing, open, gregarious, and generous with his money to boot, but perhaps he wasn't as much of a family man as he'd made himself out to be. The realization was unsettling and made me question even more strongly what he had been doing in Cape Bay.

It was clear his visit hadn't been an end-of-summer family vacation. He was here alone. He was living it up, unhindered by his wife and family obligations. He was drinking high-end alcohol and hooking up with a bar waitress he'd only just met and hadn't even given his last name to. Just two nights before, he'd been out to dinner with his wife and young son. And a day later, he was dead. Had his activities while he was away caused his death? Or was it whatever had brought him to Cape Bay in the first place? And why didn't I know what that was?

I tried to clear my mind and allow the sandman a chance to come, but it wasn't working. Something about my conversation with Suzy was bothering me. In all honesty, a lot of it bothered me, but there was something in particular I couldn't quite put my finger on. I tried to remember what it was, but my mind was going so fast over the facts of the case that I couldn't pin it down.

Just relax, Fran. You need to relax.

And there it was: *relax*. That was what had been bothering me. Suzy had said Abraham could help you "relax." Ed Martin had mentioned her saying something similar when she was at the hotel with Abraham—that she was stressed out and needed to relax. Was waitressing really so stressful?

As soon as that thought crossed my mind, I dismissed it as ridiculous. My old New York friends would ask the same thing about working at the café—is working at a coffee shop really so stressful? Yes. Yes, it was.

But I didn't go around talking about how I needed to relax. And what did Suzy mean when she said he could help her relax? Suzy didn't seem like the type to beat around the bush about much. So what was she trying to hide? Something illegal? Drugs? I knew more about drugs from watching TV than I did from personal experience, but I did remember from my middle school health teacher that some drugs were called "uppers" and "downers."

Was Suzy saying Abraham Casey had given her some kind of drug to help her relax? Even with what I'd learned about him, I had trouble fitting that idea with the straight-laced pharmacist I'd seen in so many pictures online.

Even if he was a cheating, unpre-scribed-drug-dispensing pharmacist, what was he doing in Cape Bay, and why didn't anyone know? As friendly and outgoing as he was, why hadn't he told anyone why he was in town? It seemed out of character for the man who had posted his every move online. Had his wife known where he was? Was she okay with him going off to the beach for a few days while she stayed home with their small child? He'd clearly planned the trip, but for what purpose? Did the odd scheduling have something to do with it? Was that a clue?

The answers weren't coming to me, and staying up half the night thinking about it wasn't going to help. At that point, I wasn't sure any amount of thinking would help. Suzy hadn't suggested anyone new for me to talk to, and unless I was going to contact Abraham Casey's wife, which I had no intention of doing, I was at a loss for where to go next. If I could clear my mind and fall asleep, maybe some brilliant idea would pop into my head by morning. Or maybe I would dream the answer. I wasn't optimistic.

I rolled over, laying my arm across Latte's warm little body. I felt his soft fur beneath my fingers and the steady rise and fall of his belly as he slept, completely unaware of my internal turmoil. Gradually, the comfortable rhythm of his breathing lulled me to sleep, and his tongue on my face woke me the next morning.

"Hey there, buddy," I murmured as I tried to drag myself from sleep. I scratched him behind the ears and hoped it would distract him from his true goal–breakfast. I just wanted to lie in bed a little bit longer.

I felt him shove his head under my hand and realized I must have fallen back asleep. "Okay, okay." I rolled over to check the time. It was long past time for me to get up. I pulled myself into a sitting position then stumbled downstairs to let Latte out and feed him. I went back upstairs as he ate and made my way through my morning routine.

I didn't know what to do next in my investigation of Abraham Casey's murder. It seemed as though I were at a dead end. I wondered if Mike was doing any better. I was sure he was. He was a professional at this, after all. I resolved to put the whole thing out of my mind, at least until some new piece of information fell into my lap or some previously overlooked connection appeared in my mind. Unfortunately, I wasn't very hopeful about either of those prospects.

Latte and I went for our walk, and I fixed myself a light, early lunch. One of Matt's coworkers was having a Labor Day cookout, and we were invited. Dinner was scheduled for early and promised to be large. With the likely menu of burgers, hot dogs, chips, dips, pretzels, and sweets, I knew I would be stuffed by the end of the evening. A light lunch was exactly what I needed, and I followed it with another long walk, just as a preemptive measure against the quantity of food I expected to consume later.

After the second walk, which was complemented by a rousing game of fetch and an extended race around the playing fields, I showered and changed into cookout clothes–shorts, a T-shirt, and a pair of sneakers. I was inspired by Matt's warning that a game of softball was likely to break out sometime during the afternoon.

He picked me up promptly at three o'clock and drove us to his coworker's house in the next town.

"So, whose house is it we're going to again?" I asked as we cruised out of Cape Bay.

"His name's Brant. I've worked with him for about five years."

"And his wife?"

"Mindy."

"What does she do?"

"Not sure. Something medical, I think."

"'Something medical.' You've worked with the guy for five years, and you don't know what his wife does?"

He shrugged as he kept his eyes on the road. "Doesn't really come up."

I sighed. "Are they from here?"

Matt thought for a minute. "I don't think so."

"Where are they from?"

"I'm not sure. It's not something that has come up."

I rolled my eyes and wondered if this was what Dawn felt like when she was talking to me—like she was speaking to someone from another planet whose customs were nothing like her own. Customs like actually speaking to your coworkers about their lives and families. "Kids?" I asked.

"Yes."

"Are you sure? That's something that actually came up?"

"He has pictures of them at his desk."

I wanted to ask if he was sure the kids were Brant's and not nieces and nephews or much-younger siblings but decided that particular line of questioning would serve no purpose but to frustrate me, and in all likelihood, the pictures probably were of Brant's kids.

Brant and Mindy did not have kids.

I was getting fresh lemonade from the pretty, excessively decorated glass drink dispenser that even had lemon slices floating in it when Mindy came up.

"Are you enjoying yourself?" She flashed a gorgeous smile with brilliant white teeth. She was impeccably dressed in a white sleeveless collared top, white tennis skirt, and white tennis shoes. I was reasonably certain her skirt and top had been ironed more recently than they'd been worn to play tennis. Mindy's long, lush brown hair was pulled into a high ponytail.

"I am." I felt woefully underdressed. "The lemonade is delicious." I tried not to be jealous.

"Thanks, my mom made it." She gestured in the direction of an immaculately groomed older woman, who looked and was dressed just like Mindy, except her hair was shorter and shining white. "I have no culinary skills whatsoever."

I chuckled and was secretly glad I at least had one thing up on her.

"The outfits are also all my mom. Her twist on white not being worn after Labor Day is that it's the only color that actually can be worn on Labor Day." Perhaps Mindy wasn't quite as perfect as I thought.

"Are those your kids over there?" I gestured with my lemonade glass, which managed to be frosty cold despite the end-of-summer heat, at a group of kids running around who were also dressed in immaculate white. I suspected their clothes would stop being white long before the party ended.

"Oh God, no!" Mindy exclaimed. "Nooo. No, no, no. No kids for me."

"Are they Brant's?" I thought perhaps they were her stepchildren, and her mother insisted on them also being dressed in white.

"No." She looked confused. "They're my sister's. Brant and I don't have kids."

"But Matt—" I started then stopped, realizing what had happened. "Matt's an idiot."

"Let me guess, no clue about any of his coworkers' personal lives beyond the most basic details?"

"Not a one." I paused. "Your name is Mindy, right?" I dreaded the answer.

She laughed. "Sure is. And you're Franny?"

"Well, most people call me Fran. Or Francesca. Whichever. Franny's fine, too, though."

"Men." she laughed again. "You're a chef?"

"I own a coffee shop. Antonia's Italian Café, over in Cape Bay."

"Oh, I love that place! The best coffee I've ever had. And your desserts! Seriously, I wish I could bake like that."

"We bring most of it in. I've been known to make a cupcake or two, though."

"Still jealous." She smiled.

"Matt said you do something medical?"

"Pharmacist."

My heart skipped a beat. I forced myself to focus on the lovely conversation I was having with Mindy and not on the other pharmacist who'd recently been occupying my thoughts.

"That must be interesting."

"It is. Although you wouldn't know it from the convention I just came from."

"Convention?"

"Pharmacist convention over in Providence. I genuinely love learning about new medications and reading the literature, but, my God, the presentations were boring. I hardly even know why I go except to see a couple old friends I rarely get to catch up with."

"You said you just came from it?"

"Well, I got back Saturday afternoon. Drove out to Providence on Wednesday, had a reception that night, seminars all day Thursday and Friday, a couple more Saturday morning, then came home. I thought about just driving over there every day instead of staying in the hotel, but it's just far enough that I didn't want to do that, you know?"

I nodded absently. Wednesday through Saturday. She'd gone to Providence for a pharmacy convention and stayed from Wednesday through Saturday. The same days Abraham Casey, the pharmacist, had been booked at the Seaside Inn.

I wondered if that was the excuse he'd given his wife for his trip out of town. It made so much sense. What better excuse? And it would have been easier than years ago when she would have caught on if she called the hotel and he wasn't there. No, she would just call his cell phone, which he could answer from, and say he was, anywhere.

"You don't happen to know a guy named Abraham Casey, do you? He's a pharmacist, too. I think he was supposed to be at that convention, now that you've mentioned it." I felt safe saying his name without her connecting it to the body in the alley in Cape Bay. It hadn't been printed in the paper yet—neither the Boston paper nor the local one—and as far as I knew, it wasn't public knowledge.

Mindy thought for a moment. "No, can't say I do. Is he a friend of yours?"

"An acquaintance. Just thought it was worth a shot asking. It's a small world and all, you know?"

"Oh, I know. You wouldn't believe the connections I make—I once filled prescriptions for years for a woman before I found out she was the wife of my very first boyfriend back in middle school. It's always worth asking."

"Well, I'm glad that you don't think I'm crazy."

"Not at all. Crazy is making your thirty-five-year-old daughter dress in tennis whites even though she hasn't picked up a racket in almost twenty years."

"Mindy! Franny!" someone called. We both looked up in the direction the voice had come from. Brant was standing across the lawn waving his hands over his head, a softball bat in one and a glove in the other.

Matt was beside him also waving his arms in the air. "Softball!"

"So much for relaxing in the shade," Mindy said. She dropped her glass into a bucket of soapy water and motioned for me to do the same.

"Do you have enough glasses to get through the day?" I wondered who had that

216

many glasses and how they kept up with the dishes.

"More than enough. Mom rents them and pays her friend's granddaughter to wash them and cycle them through the freezer throughout the day."

"Wow." I was impressed at the effort her mother made for what was otherwise your average Labor Day cookout.

"Yeah, wow."

As we headed across the field toward where Matt and Brant were trying to figure out how to anchor a paper plate to the grass so it could serve as home plate, I thought about the remarkable coincidence of Mindy being a pharmacist and virtually laying out Abraham Casey's excuse for getting out of town.

Chapter Sixteen

"Looked like you were having a good time with Mindy," Matt said as we drove back to Cape Bay.

"I did!" I was pleased to realize I meant it. After our talk about the pharmacy convention, we'd chatted for the rest of the evening, laughing through the softball game about how useless we were as we swung and missed balls our significant others said we should have hit, and we failed to come within roughly a mile of balls hit in our direction in the field. We were both pretty sure we would have gotten kicked out of the game if they'd had enough players to replace us.

"What'd you two talk about?"

"A little of everything. How useless you and Brant are at accurately learning and sharing personal information about each other. Fun fact: they do not have any children."

"They don't?"

"No, they don't."

"Then who were all those kids running around?"

"Really, Matty?"

"What?" he asked innocently.

"They belonged to any of the other people who were there."

"Yeah, I guess."

I gave up and decided to bring up the other significant piece of information I'd acquired. "Anyway, Mindy is a pharmacist."

"Oh yeah? I thought it was something medical."

"She went to a pharmacy convention this week. Wednesday through Saturday."

"Sounds dull."

"She said it was." I paused and waited to see if he'd figure out what I was getting at.

When he didn't, I chose to be glad he was paying more attention to the road than to what I was trying to tell him, as the alternative would probably not turn out well for anyone. "Can you think of anyone else who's a pharmacist?"

"Um, I think my pharmacist's name is Bill or something. Bob maybe."

"Anyone else?"

"Who am I supposed to be thinking of?" He clearly did not have much patience for my quizzing. Again, I chose to see it as a good thing.

"Maybe someone who was found in an alley?"

"Casey?"

"You got it."

"Did she know him or something?"

I decided to lay it all out for him. Trying to get him to figure the whole thing out was going to exhaust my patience. "I think the conference she went to was what he used as a cover story for his wife. The dates line up perfectly. Ed Martin said he booked his room three months ago, which is about the time you'd register for a conference."

"How do you know he didn't actually go to the conference? Maybe he just doesn't like staying at the same hotel as everybody else."

"Providence is an hour and a half away, Matty. It's closer to Boston than it is to Cape Bay."

"So why would he even book a hotel? Why not stay at home and just drive down every day?"

"That's the point. What if he told his wife he was going to the conference and had to stay there so he could network or go to all the activities or whatever? At the conferences I've been to, interacting with your peers is more valuable than the actual sessions. Besides, would you want to drive from Boston to Providence in time for a session at eight in the morning?"

Matt visibly cringed at the thought of the traffic that would be involved. There was a reason he didn't live in the city even though he could easily have gotten a more lucrative job in Boston than the one he had. It wasn't as though Bostonians were particularly known for their superior driving skills, and anyone who both lived and worked in the city would take public transportation if they needed to commute farther than they could walk. No, travelling from Boston to Providence and back again each day for a conference was a ridiculous idea. And so was travelling from Cape Bay to Providence.

"Okay, you have a point," Matt conceded. "But why did he come here? If he was using the conference as a cover, he could have gone anywhere."

"I don't know," I admitted. "But I have a feeling whatever it was is what got him killed."

"You sure it wasn't his wife? She found out that he wasn't at the conference after all and came after him?"

"Just for going on vacation without her? There would have to be more. I mean, you couldn't blame her for confronting him, but killing him? Seems a bit much."

"What if he got violent, and she fought back? Self-defense?" he suggested.

"So she shot him and made it look like a suicide to cover it up? I don't know."

"Think about it—they have a kid, right?"

"Yeah."

"If she kills him, she goes to jail, and then what happens to the kid? Besides, you can't benefit from a life insurance policy if you cause the death."

I turned my head slowly to look at him. "And why do you know that?"

He grinned. "TV. I swear."

"I hope so." I settled back in my seat. I thought over Matt's suggestion. It seemed plausible. It was one of the first theories we'd had—a lovers' quarrel. Since I'd found out about Abraham's rendezvous with Suzy, it seemed even more plausible. Maybe Leah Casey had found out her husband lied about going to the conference then came to Cape Bay to confront him. Maybe she caught him with Suzy. Maybe she confronted him. Maybe she was so angry she killed him. Or maybe he got violent when she confronted him, and she defended herself. Matt's points about jail and insurance both seemed valid.

I wondered if I should call Mike and fill him in on what I'd learned. I didn't really want him to know I'd blatantly disregarded his direction not to get involved, but I couldn't very well keep information from him that could be critical to solving a murder. It had been one thing when I had some lingering questions—who the victim was, who killed him, why they killed him, why they arranged it to look like a suicide.

I hadn't meant to go this far. I had just been curious and had a few questions. Mike would likely be furious if I came clean, but I didn't see what choice I had. For all I knew, withholding information was a crime of its own. Maybe that's what my mother had meant when she said "curiosity killed the cat." Once I gave in to my curiosity, I was doomed no matter what.

Matt parked the car in his driveway and walked me home. He stood with me while Latte ran around the yard, then kissed me goodnight. Latte and I went up to bed. I expected to be up again half the night thinking about what I was going to do with my information, but apparently now that my questions had all been answered, my brain and body were both ready for rest. My head had barely hit the pillow when I fell sound asleep.

I woke up early the next morning, knowing I had a big day ahead of me. I had an exercise class, a haircut, work, and a night out with Sammy. Somewhere in there, I had to contact Mike Stanton and fill him in on everything I'd learned. I took solace in the fact that even though he might be mad at me, he probably couldn't arrest me.

Latte and I hurried through our morning routine, leaving me just enough time to walk to the gym before my class started. I was taking a kickboxing class, something I'd long resisted. I'd never liked all the hitting and kicking involved. It felt too aggressive, even if it was just a punching bag I was attacking. I preferred to alleviate my stress by curling up on the couch with a nice glass of red wine. I wondered if I should recommend that method of relaxation to Suzy but decided she was probably familiar with the effects of alcohol.

The young, perky front desk clerk at the local gym had extolled the virtues of kick-boxing, encouraging me to sign up, even if just for one month to see how I liked it. When I declined, she suggested water aerobics. I signed up for kickboxing. After I'd paid for the class, I wondered if she had deliberately manipulated me into it. But since I was already signed up, and I'd only committed to a single month, I stuck with it and eventually even found that I liked it. Perky Karli smiled every time I walked past her on my way to class, and she was kind enough not to say anything when I signed up for a second month.

After kickboxing, I headed home to take a shower. I felt slightly ridiculous washing my hair less than an hour before paying someone to do it for me, but I couldn't handle the thought of going into Beach Waves with sweaty, gross hair. It was a catch-22. I could get a shower before I got my hair done and have someone rewash my already clean hair, or I could wait and shower after my cut and ruin the blowout with the humidity. Double washing my hair was less of a blow to my dignity.

After my shower, I went ahead and put on my work clothes so I didn't have to come back home. I took Latte out and threw his tennis ball for him a few times. I felt the lightest and happiest I had in days. Abraham Casey's murder was all but solved, I had drinks with Sammy to look forward to, and I was finally getting my hair cut. I must have gotten carried away with Latte because by the time I checked the time, I was running late.

"Here you go!" I sang, giving Latte a treat. "Love you! See you later!" I let him lick me on the nose a few times then shut the door and headed for the salon.

"Hi. Fran Amaro," I said as I stepped up to the front desk.

The pink-and-purple-haired girl staffing the counter made me wonder exactly where we found so many bored teenagers in such a small town. Then I realized it was the first day of school, and instead of sitting in a classroom, she was sitting in a salon, so she had to be older than I thought. I wondered whether I was just getting too old to accurately guess the ages of people younger than me. The thought was not encouraging, especially knowing another birthday was on the horizon.

The girl looked at me blankly.

"I have an appointment." I tried to be polite.

"Who with?"

With whom, I mentally corrected. "Chase Williams," I said instead, deciding civility was a more important lesson for this girl than grammar.

She clicked her computer mouse a few times. "Okay, have a seat." She managed a level of monotone I hadn't realized possible.

I took a chair and picked up a magazine featuring a celebrity wedding on the cover. It was at least a few months old because I happened to know the couple was already divorced. Still, I flipped through it, looking for my favorite feature, "What's In Your Bag?" where they emptied out a celebrity's purse and took a picture, then annotated the contents with prices and some inane bit of information about why the product was in the celebrity's bag. "She loves this lip balm ($25 for 0.25 oz.) for how silky soft it makes her lips!" "Q-tips ($2 for 250) are a must for quick makeup fixes on the go!" "This luxurious hand crème ($225 for 0.75 oz.) is essential for maintaining the health of her nails and cuticles! Use it to smooth flyaways, too!" I couldn't say whether I loved seeing the products or the prices more.

"Fran?" an assistant asked, poking her head around a corner.

"That's me!" I stood up and reluctantly parted with the magazine. I hadn't yet gotten to the "Who Wore It Best?" feature, which was another favorite. I saw the assistant's face as it went from a happy smile to a look of concern as she saw my still-wet hair wrapped up in a bun.

She politely waited until I was next to her before she commented. "You know you don't have to wash your own hair. We do that for you."

"I know. I had a kickboxing class this morning and–"

"Oh, say no more! I totally understand!"

She took me to the shampoo bowl and rewashed my hair. At least the salon's products were high quality and didn't make my hair feel as dry and awful as the cheap stuff. She finished with a quick scalp massage, wrung the excess water out of my hair, and led me to Chase's chair.

"Have you ever been here before?"

"Nope, first time."

"You're in for a treat. Chase's haircuts are amazing."

Chapter Seventeen

Chase stood behind me, flipping my hair, which had been cut, dried, and styled, over my shoulders, pulling it back, tucking it behind my ears, and tousling it up. "Do you like it?" he asked.

I nodded. "My head feels so light!"

"Shake your head. Run your fingers through it. See how it feels."

I did as instructed. "It's so soft." I thought it was probably the best haircut I'd ever had, better even than the astronomically expensive ones I'd had in New York. It was exactly what I wanted—what I'd already had, but better.

He flipped it back and forth again then rested his hands on my shoulders as he looked at me in the mirror. "It was so nice to finally get the chance to catch up with you."

"I know! It's been forever, hasn't it?" As long as it had been, he hadn't changed a bit over the years. He still had the same sandy blond hair and the same pale blue eyes. Admittedly, the stubble on his chin hadn't been there in high school, but whenever I'd seen him in passing since then, it had grazed his face. He'd grown taller and broader since school, but the grin was still the same, as was the easy surfer-dude voice and the laid-back mannerisms. At his core, he was the same old Chase even after more than fifteen years.

"Probably high school since we've had a real conversation."

"You know, you're probably right."

"I think every time I come into the café, you're so busy. I see you behind the counter, making drinks for everyone, rushing around. It's not stressing you out too much, is it, Fran? Too much stress isn't good for you."

I was touched by his concern. I'd always felt having my hair done was like a form of therapy—you come in, sit down for an hour, talk to a professional, and when you leave, you feel fresh and rejuvenated. Like yourself, only better. And stylists like Chase only proved the point. Not only was he great at doing hair, he was great at reading his clients.

"I'm doing okay." I smiled at him in the mirror. "We have our busy times, but we have our slow time, too. You just always seem to come in when there's a rush."

"Don't I know it," he laughed. He touched the ends of my hair again, arranging them just so. "But, you know, seriously, Fran, if you ever get to feeling like it's too much, let me know. I have some stuff that can help you relax a little."

"What? Like scissors and a comb? Haircuts do always make me feel better." I laughed nervously. I was almost certain that wasn't what he meant.

"Well, there's that," he laughed. "But I meant I have something else. To help you relax." He paused and looked at me for a second. I tried to keep my face perfectly neutral. "Just let me know, okay?"

I nodded and tried to give him a little bit of a smile. Not enough to encourage him, but enough to let him know I wasn't going to run straight to the police to turn him in for offering me...whatever he had just offered. Drugs? A gift certificate for a massage? Essential oils?

As we walked toward the front counter, I chided myself for assuming the worst. Chase could quite possibly be offering me some kind of herbal supplement. Matt or Sammy could have said the exact same thing, and I never would have questioned it. The situation with Abraham Casey had me jumping to crazy conclusions. I needed to find Mike as soon as possible and fill him in on everything I'd learned over the past few days so I could get back to my normal life and stop assuming my friends were trying to sell me drugs.

"I'll check her out," Chase said to the bored, punk-haired teenager at the desk.

"Whatever." She sighed and rolled her chair back from the computer.

Chase leaned over the computer and punched a few buttons. "I'll give you the friends and family discount." He winked at me. He clicked the mouse a couple of times and told me the price. The salon's rates were already reasonable, especially in comparison to what I was used to paying, but the number Chase gave me was a forty-percent discount on top of that. I tipped him generously in exchange.

I was giving him a quick hug goodbye when I glanced out the window and saw Mike on the other side of the street, walking down the sidewalk in the direction of the salon. It was perfect timing. I could go talk to him, tell him everything, and still make it to work on time. I waved goodbye to Chase and hurried outside to catch up with Mike. I stepped out between the parallel-parked cars and glanced down the street to check for oncoming traffic. It was all clear, so I crossed to the median.

"Mike!" I called out, waving my hand as he passed me across the other lane of traffic. "Mike!"

He stopped in front of the miniature golf place and turned around to see who was calling him. His face grew stern when he saw it was me. I wondered if he'd heard about my investigation.

"Hi, Mike!" I caught up to him on the sidewalk. He was wearing a suit and tie–his detective clothes. When he was just patrolling the streets, he wore a regular uniform. The fact that he was wearing his investigating clothes didn't bode well for me.

"Hello, Francesca." Whatever he looked so serious about wasn't good if he was using my full name.

"How are you?" I tried to sound cheerful.

"I've been better. In fact, I was better this morning before I went over to the Seaside Inn to interview Ed Martin."

I swallowed hard and tried to play off my apprehension. "Oh, did it not go well?"

"It went very well, actually. His recollection of the events in question was quite good. Apparently, someone came by the other day and helped refresh everything for him."

"Oh?"

"Fran..." The warning tone in his voice unmistakable.

"Yes?"

"I told you to stay out of it."

"I know. I'm sorry. I didn't mean to get involved."

"But you did."

I nodded.

"You need to tell me everything."

"Can we go somewhere to talk? Instead of...out here?" I waved my hand around to indicate the very public nature of Main Street. The idea of going into detail about my findings while standing where anyone could walk by and hear me was incredibly unappealing, as was the idea of enduring Mike's reaction.

"You mean like my interrogation room?" he suggested.

"I was thinking more like my café."

Mike grunted, turned, and stalked off in the direction of the coffee shop. I took that to mean he was agreeing to my suggestion and followed him.

He pulled open the café door and let me go in first.

"Hey!" Sammy exclaimed. "You're here early. I didn't expect you for—" She stopped suddenly when she saw Mike and his sullen expression. "Hey, Mike." She barely succeeded at sounding cheerful.

I made a move to sit in an armchair in the corner, but Mike had other ideas. "Back room," he barked as he blew past me. He managed to flash a smile at Sammy. "Black coffee, please, Sam. Large. And could you bring it to me in the back?"

"Sure thing, Mike." She raised her eyebrows and made her eyes big as I walked past her. The code for both was "what did you do" and "you're in trouble."

I grimaced and followed Mike into the back. He shut the door behind us and sat in a chair. He crossed his legs, ankle over knee, and folded his arms across his chest. He was a tall, muscular man, quite imposing in the small room. I edged past him and sat down in another chair facing him.

He didn't say a word, which only served to make me more nervous. He kept his eyes on me, and I waited. There was a knock on the door.

"Come in," Mike called.

"I have your coffee." Sammy stuck her head in.

"Thanks, Sam." He reached up and took the coffee from her without breaking eye contact with me.

Sammy mouthed "good luck" and slipped back out, pulling the door closed.

Mike took a sip of his coffee. "You may as well get started," he said.

"Well, that night—the night of the murder—"

"I'm sorry?" Mike interrupted me.

"The night of the murder."

He leaned forward and put an elbow on his knee. "How do you know that?"

"Know what?"

"I told you it was a suicide. Why did you just say murder?"

"Oh, um, I just sort of...figured it out. Suicide didn't make sense to me, so I thought it was probably a murder."

"Suicide didn't make sense to you." He shook his head. "Go on."

"Well, that was the first thing. I went home and talked to Matt about it and realized it was probably a murder. So the next day, I went and talked to Mary Ellen to see what she could tell me about Abraham Casey."

"Wait, how did you find out his name?"

"Mary Ellen."

"Mary Ellen told you?"

I nodded. "Is that not okay? She didn't know if it was okay or not."

"It's not okay when she's giving you information she's withholding from the police."

"But—she wasn't withholding it. She told you as soon as she remembered she knew it."

"And what makes you think that?"

"She told me."

"When?"

"Saturday."

"*Saturday?*"

"Yes. She told me she remembered it during the night and called the officer who interviewed her first thing in the morning. She left him a message."

Mike stared at me for a second. "Son of a—" he muttered under his breath, followed by another, even less polite word. "She called Bradshaw?" he asked in a normal tone of voice.

"That's what she said. He didn't get the message?"

"He either didn't get it or just didn't bother to tell anyone. Do you know how many hours we wasted trying to figure out this guy's name when we could have had it first thing?"

A horrible thought occurred to me. "You don't think Mary Ellen lied to me about calling, do you?"

"I don't think so. I've had issues with Bradshaw before. Never like this, though." He shook his head, and I could tell he was trying to contain himself. "How did Mary Ellen know his name?"

"It was on his credit card receipt."

"He paid with a credit card?"

"Yes."

"He paid with a credit card," he repeated, seemingly pained by the words. Mike leaned back in his chair and rubbed his forehead vigorously. "I'm going to fire him," he said, again under his breath. "He's fired. I'm firing him."

"So, wait—if you didn't get Mary Ellen's message, how did you find out his name?"

"His fingerprints came back from IAFIS yesterday." He must have noticed the blank look on my face. "Integrated Automated Fingerprint Identification System. It's an FBI system. Lets you compare a set of fingerprints against a huge pool of them. Casey had to get fingerprinted to get his pharmacy license." He paused. "I assume you already know he was a pharmacist." He sounded weary.

I nodded.

"Of course you do. You're a better detective than half the guys on my force, and it's not even your job." He pointed to me. "Don't you ever tell anyone I said that."

I grinned. "I won't."

"Tell me what else you know." He pulled a little notebook out of his pocket. He flipped to a blank page and poised his pencil over it.

I ran quickly through the other information I'd gathered during my nearly three-day head start—his wife and child, the pharmacists' convention, and my conversation with Suzy. Mike scribbled down notes as I spoke.

"So, you think there's a drug angle to this?" Mike asked.

"I don't know if I think there's a drug angle. I think there are maybe some drugs involved. Lovers' quarrel makes the most sense to me, though. His wife found out he didn't go to the conference, came here to confront him, caught him with Suzy, and things got violent."

"So you think the wife did it? What's her name..." He flipped the pages in his little notebook, looking for her name.

"Leah," I offered.

"Of course you know that."

I smiled. He didn't. I guessed he was still annoyed his officer had dropped the ball.

"You think Leah Casey did it?"

"I'm not really *sure* she did it." I didn't want him to think I had more evidence than I did pointing in her direction. "And even if she did, it could have been self-defense. He might have attacked her first."

"And have you spoken with Mrs. Casey?"

"No! Of course not. I'm not going to call up a grieving widow and start asking her questions about her dead husband."

"If you'd called her before last night, you would have been the one breaking the news to her."

I cringed, grateful I'd decided not to contact her. "I'll leave that stuff up to you. I'm not the police, remember?"

"Oh, I remember. I'm just not so sure you do."

I looked down at my hands in my lap.

"So, since you seem to know everything about this case, can you tell me why he didn't actually go to the conference? He was registered, you know."

I didn't know, and I could have kicked myself for not having thought to check whether he'd been registered. "I figure he just wanted a break from his everyday life. He probably booked the conference so he'd have a cover and then decided to just go to the beach for a few days, get away from it all."

"Hook up with a waitress he met in a bar," Mike added. "Anything else you've noticed? Anything that seemed unusual?"

"No, I think I've told you everything."

Mike nodded and drummed the eraser of his pencil against his notebook. He looked as though he was thinking hard about something. "Well, Fran, I have to tell you, you've done some good work here. I still don't approve." He looked at me pointedly. "But it's good work. The lovers' quarrel is a solid theory. I gotta say, though—I think there might be a little more to it than that." He shifted forward in his chair and looked at me. "We've known for a while that there are drugs coming into Cape Bay. Not street drugs. Pharmaceuticals. We've been keeping it quiet until we could put the pieces of the puzzle together. Not just who's selling it here but how they're getting it in. With Casey being a pharmacist and Suzy hinting that he had drugs he was sharing, I don't think we should dismiss the drug angle just yet."

Chapter Eighteen

Mike and I sat in the back room and talked about the case for a few more minutes. He told me about all the proper procedures they'd followed, and I told him about all the gut instincts and logical leaps I'd followed. He shook his head every time I told him about something I'd figured out on my own that had taken the police department way more time to learn.

He finished his coffee and tossed the paper cup in the trash. "I guess I'd better get going. I have some leads I have to follow and an officer I have to chew out."

"Good luck with both of those. I'd tell you not to be too hard on Officer Bradshaw, but he probably deserves it."

"Damn right he does. Could have blown the whole investigation. And it wasn't just not relaying the message from Mary Ellen—he shouldn't have needed to get the message in the first place. He should have asked to see the receipt when he was there Friday night." He shook his head, obviously disgusted with the incompetence of his officer. "I can't believe we had to wait three days to get information we should have had immediately."

"I feel bad. I mean, if I had called you Saturday to let you know—"

"To let us know information you thought we already had? That's not your fault, Fran. You had no way of knowing we—well, one of us, anyway—would overlook something so obvious."

"Besides, you probably would have shut me down right then."

"You better believe it. Not that it probably would have done much good."

I shrugged then nodded. "Probably not."

Mike shook his head at me. "Well, thanks for the information, Fran. If you think of anything else or come across anything at all, even if you think we already know—"

"I'll call you right away."

"That's not an invitation to do any more investigating."

"I know. And I'm done, anyway. I've had enough of this case."

"I hope so." He reached to open the door.

"One thing—"

"I'm not even out the door, Fran!"

"I know!" I smiled sheepishly. "But how did you find out it wasn't a suicide? I assume it was based on more than a feeling you had."

"Autopsy. No gunshot residue on his hands. And the bullet's angle of entry was wrong. Straight on instead of at an angle." He twisted his hand to show how hard it would be to shoot yourself dead on.

"So it wasn't hard to figure out?"

"Not once we had the medical examiner's opinion. Whoever did it is either not very good at murder or was just hoping to get a couple days' head start on us."

"Anybody see Leah Casey in the past few days?"

"That's what I'm about to go check with Boston PD on. They did the death notification."

"Well, good luck."

"Thanks. The way this case has been going, I'm going to need it." He opened the door and let me precede him into the café.

A few customers were scattered around enjoying their drinks and, from the looks of most of the tables, their lunches. Most of the people were locals, a stark difference from the crowd that had filled the place a week ago. I had a sneaking suspicion a lot of the locals avoided spending much time in the shops during the tourist season, preferring to wait for the calm of the off-season and the company of each other.

Sammy was leaning over the counter, talking to someone I couldn't see. I almost couldn't believe my ears when I heard her laugh. She sounded so happy and carefree. I angled my head as I walked around the counter to see who she was talking to.

"Leary! What are you doing here?" I heard Mike call.

Finally reaching where I could see who Sammy was talking to, I saw Mike shake Ryan Leary's hand and slap him on the back.

"Hey, Mike!" Ryan replied. "Just stopped in for some coffee and a bite to eat before my shift."

"Come by and see me when you get into the office. I have some new information about the case I want to share with you."

"Yes, sir. I should be there in an hour or so."

Mike nodded and turned back to the counter. Before he could even ask, Sammy handed him a large to-go cup and a bag that probably contained his usual of a mozzarella-tomato-basil sandwich and a piece of tiramisu.

"You know me too well," Mike said with a smile. "Thanks, Sam. Thanks to you, too, Fran."

"What's a guy gotta do to get that kind of service?" Ryan asked as Mike walked away.

"You gotta come in a lot. Like, a lot," Sammy said. I saw a twinkle in her eye that hadn't been there for weeks. "How often does Mike come in, Fran?"

"Few times a week!" Mike called from the door.

"More than that!" I retorted.

"Don't tell my wife!" He pushed the door open and waved once before he disappeared down the sidewalk.

"Almost every day," I said to Ryan. I looked at Sammy for confirmation. She nodded vigorously.

"I might be able to manage that," Ryan said. "The food's good. The drinks are great. The company couldn't be better. I could get used to coming around." He flashed a brilliant smile our way.

"We could get used to having you," Sammy said with a smile. She was good at engaging customers, connecting with them, and charming them into coming back, not just for the coffee, but also for the pleasant company.

The bell over the door jingled as a customer came in.

"I'll get her," I said before Sammy could even look up. She seemed happy talking to Ryan, and I knew happiness was something she needed right now.

I got the customer's drink, and the next, and the next. We had a slow but steady stream of customers, enough to keep from getting bored but not so many that it was overwhelming. The café started to empty out, Ryan left, and Sammy joined me at the register.

"Sorry about that," she said. "We just kind of got started talking, then you seemed like you were handling it and—"

"You're fine." I cut her off. "You were enjoying yourself, and I had everything under control. You do enough around here. You're entitled to slack off a little every now and then."

Sammy looked uncomfortable. She was a hard worker and a perfectionist, and she didn't like the suggestion that she wasn't working her hardest. She worked incredibly hard the vast majority of the time, which earned her a chat or two with a customer, especially since I was there to take care of the café's patrons.

A pair of customers got up, and Sammy hurried to clear their table before I could so much as flinch in their direction. I hadn't intended to guilt her into working even harder than usual, but apparently, I had done just that. I'd have to avoid the words "slack off" the next time I said something like that to her.

The café gradually emptied out, and Sammy and I found ourselves alone.

"You can go home if you want," I offered. "I don't think it'll be too busy the rest of the day."

"Okay, thanks." But Sammy didn't make a move for the door. She just stood at the counter, swaying slightly, and not quite making eye contact with me.

"What?" I asked finally, deciding there was something on her mind she didn't want to bring up.

"What happened back there with Mike? When you two went back there, he looked furious, but by the time you came out, the two of you were laughing and joking. What happened?"

I ran through the morning's conversation with Mike briefly for Sammy—how angry he was that I had been investigating the case, how his officer's major screw-up had basically gotten me off the hook, and some of the information I had shared with him, including my theory that Leah Casey, the victim's wife, was somehow involved.

"Wow," Sammy said. "You're like a regular part of the police force now."

"Well, I wouldn't say that, and Mike defi-nitely wouldn't. I think it's more that he was just glad that I had a little information he could use."

"Mm-hmm, sure," Sammy teased. "He's going to call you up and hire you tomorrow. 'Fran, I know you're busy with the coffee shop and all, but we've had a rash of people waking up to their lawn ornaments being rearranged, and I need your expertise.'" Sammy lowered her voice and did her best impression of Mike's gruff cop demeanor. It was terrible and hilarious.

"I can only hope Cape Bay's crime goes back to just having that kind of stuff."

"I know, right?" Something outside caught Sammy's eye, and she reached around her back to untie her apron. "Still okay if I head out?"

"Do you see any more customers than we had ten minutes ago?"

"Nope." She pulled her apron over her head. "Are we still on for tonight? Drinks at Fiesta Mexicana?" She was headed for the back room, barely glancing at me as she spoke.

"Yeah, of course. Where are you going?"

"Home. I just–remembered I had something I had to do. I'll see you tonight. Bye!" She grabbed her purse and disappeared out the back door so fast I barely understood what was going on.

Just as the back door closed, the front door opened. I put on a big smile to greet the customer and turned around, immediately realizing why Sammy had suddenly hurried out.

"Francesca!" Mrs. D'Angelo exclaimed. "Oh, Francesca, how are you?" Mrs. D'Angelo, as unfamiliar with boundaries as ever, came around the corner and enveloped me with her arms and her heavy floral perfume. "It's been ages since I've seen you!"

"Actually, Mrs. D'Angelo, I saw you just last week. Remember? You came in." Mrs. D'Angelo's visits were a predictable weekly occurrence. I tried to refresh her memory about her last visit, but for that to work, she'd have to stop talking long enough to hear what I was saying. With Mrs. D'Angelo, that was unlikely.

"You look tired! Are you sleeping well, dear? Of course not, how could you when there are bodies turning up all over town? It's awful, just awful, isn't it? And the last one so close to your shop! Just down the street! Why, it must be just terrible for business. Just look around! There's no one here!"

"Well, it's the off-season now, so things are a little slower. We had a good crowd a little while ago, though." I knew it was useless to really get a word in, but I had to try. I couldn't just stand there.

"Oh, dear, you know it will be all right. Antonia's has been here for fifty years now–"

"It's actually closer to seventy, Mrs. D'Angelo."

"It's weathered far worse storms than this, and I'd venture that it will weather plenty more. You have a good head on your shoulders, dear. Your mother and your grandparents raised you well! You will survive this!"

The bell rang, and a customer came in. I wanted to go to the register to help him, but Mrs. D'Angelo held me fast, her sharp red nails pressing into the flesh of my upper arms. I managed a glance over my shoulder and a weak smile before Mrs. D'Angelo pulled me into another hug.

"You will survive, Francesca!" She pushed me back at arm's length, keeping her nails firmly implanted in my skin, and stared into my face. "I see your grandmother in you. You have her strength." She nodded once then released me. I reflexively rubbed the sore spots on my upper arms. "Now, is Samantha here? I heard she and that boy she was with split up, and I wanted to give her some words of encouragement."

I happened to know that Mrs. D'Angelo had already offered Sammy quite a few words of encouragement in the weeks since her breakup. "Oh, you just missed her. I'll tell her you stopped by, though."

"Please do, dear." She glanced at the delicate gold watch on her slim wrist. "My heavens! I have to go. Now that the busy season is over, the Ladies' Auxiliary is planning a trip up the coast to look for potential sister cities for Cape Bay, and I have to work out all the sleeping arrangements."

"Aren't sister cities usually overseas?" I went against my own better judgment by asking her a question when she was already halfway out the door.

"Yes, but we think it would be lovely to have some in New England so we can all be closer. Goodbye, dear! Remember, you will survive!" She breezed out the door, leaving only the scent of perfume in her wake.

Chapter Nineteen

I finished my shift without too much trouble. People wandered in throughout the afternoon, enjoyed their drinks and snacks, then headed off to wherever they were going next. The after-school rush returned with the first day of school but was sort of the anti-rush. Kids as young as elementary schoolers stopped in on their walks home. They all took their time studying the menu, inevitably choosing something either frozen and fruity or chocolatey.

A few tried to show how mature they were and ordered coffee. I looked at them with my eyebrow raised and my finger poised over the buttons on the register until they, afraid the all-powerful grown-up would tell on them to their parents, corrected themselves and requested something more age appropriate. I didn't bother telling them that I didn't recognize most of them enough to know who their parents were. The silent threat was enough.

The teenagers who came through were less adorable. They ordered their complicated drinks with multiple additions and modifications in the most disaffected, blasé tones they could muster, desperately trying to show me and their friends how impossibly cool they were. I didn't tell any of them that the harder they tried, the less cool they actually looked.

Becky came through with a group of her friends, greeted me with a bright smile, and ordered directly from the menu. Most of her friends ended up being friendlier than the vast majority of their peers.

The after-school rush bled into the dinner rush. Maybe twenty or thirty people stopped in, mostly single adults who wanted to pick up something quick and light for dinner on their way home from work. A few people stayed and ate at a table, some took their orders to go, and all of them were gone by closing time.

I straightened up the café, washed dishes, restocked the display cases, and made sure all the chairs were arranged properly at the tables. I wiped everything down and swept up so the café would be ready for Sammy the next morning.

At the last second, I remembered I had promised to bring dinner to Matt. I grabbed a bag and slid a sandwich and salad inside. Then I put one of his favorite chocolate cupcakes in a to-go box and laid it carefully on top of the other food items.

It felt luxurious to lock up an hour early. It wasn't even completely dark out when I turned the key in the door and left the café behind.

Sammy and I had planned to meet a little later so I'd have time to change and take care of Latte. I had arranged to bring the dog to Matt before I headed out for the night so he wouldn't be lonely. Latte, that was, not Matt. Although I supposed Matt probably appreciated the company as well.

Latte dashed out to greet me as soon as I opened the door. I bent down to scratch his ears and give him a good rub all over. He licked my face as though it had been more than a few hours since he'd last seen me. I rubbed his head one last time and stood up.

He ran out into the yard then ran back inside, making a beeline straight for the kitchen. He stood politely next to his bowl, paw in the air, waiting for me to serve his dinner. I scooped the kibble then went upstairs to get dressed.

It took a few minutes of staring into my closet to figure out what I wanted to wear. So much of my wardrobe was black, a popular color from my New York City days, but tonight was supposed to be a fun night for Sammy, and I wanted to wear something a little brighter.

I spotted a cornflower blue shirt that had been my mother's and perfectly complemented my eyes. I pulled it on with my favorite jeans and checked out my reflection in the mirror. It was a good look, except for my hair, which I'd put back up in a chignon during the day. I let it down and shook it out around my shoulders. I ran my fingers through it a few times until it lay just right. I touched up my makeup until I was satisfied I looked girls' night out-ready then went back downstairs.

I had a message on my cell phone from Sammy.

You almost ready?

I tapped out my reply quickly.

Just have to drop Latte off at Matt's and then I'll be on my way! Looking forward to it!

I slid my phone into my purse and slung it over my shoulder. I picked up Latte's leash.

"Latte! Come here, boy!" I called, patting my leg. Latte came running, having heard the sounds he associated with going for a walk. "You're going to Matty's for a little while, okay, boy? You'll have so much fun. Yes, you will! Yes, you will!"

I didn't even bother putting the leash on him, just held it in my hand with Matt's dinner and opened the door. Latte ran out, and I locked the door behind us. Latte did a couple of laps around me, excited to be going somewhere, then fell obediently into place beside me.

I started across the Williamses' lawn. Their house was dark. It wasn't that late, so I wondered if they were out of town. They hadn't mentioned anything, but I didn't see them that often. The sun was all the way down, and it was completely dark. On our tree-lined street, the streetlights did nothing to illuminate the paths up to our houses. I walked through the grass toward

Matt's house more by memory than by anything I could see.

Now that the Casey case was all but solved and the likely murderer was long gone from Cape Bay, I didn't have the slightest inkling of fear. I only felt excitement and anticipation for my night with Sammy. Even though we saw each other every day at work, we almost never got to spend time together in a strictly social setting. This night was special and would be fun. And it was just the two of us—no Dawn to turn our night in a direction we never expected—so it should be relaxing as well.

Just as I passed by the Williamses' front door, something caught my eye at the side of their house—a movement, or a shadow the slightest bit darker than the air around it.

I hesitated, straining my eyes to see what it was. Was it a tree in the distance? A shrub at the corner of the house? I tried to picture the Williamses' landscaping, but I couldn't remember if they had a tallish shrub anywhere. I stepped forward slowly, trying to chalk whatever it was up to my overactive imagination. And then it moved. Definitely. I was sure. The shadow moved out from the corner of the house. If it was a shrub, it was on wheels.

I stopped in my tracks. Latte stopped beside me. I didn't take my eyes off the shadow, and I was certain Latte didn't either. I heard none of his usual happy noises—his panting, the jingling of his collar, his feet tramping on the grass—but I knew he was there, which meant he was just as focused on the figure as I was.

I tried to think of what to do. I couldn't see well enough to know whether it was a person, although I couldn't think of what else it might be. It wasn't moving toward me. It wasn't moving away from me. It wasn't moving in any direction at the moment. I didn't even know if it was facing me at all. I didn't know if it could see me.

The shadow moved farther out from the house. It was definitely human. I could tell by the way he or she walked. The shadow moved farther this time, stopping directly in my path. It had to see me.

A sickening feeling came over me. What if I had been completely wrong about Abraham Casey's murder? What if it was random? What if this was his murderer striking again? Would Matt find me dead in the Williamses' yard when he came to find out why I hadn't brought Latte over yet? Oh God, what if the person hurt Latte?

I still hadn't moved, keeping my eyes fixed on the shadowy figure. I thought about my options. The Williamses' house was closest, but it was dark. If no one was home, no one could help me. I could try to run to Matt's house, but I would have to run past the figure. The shadow was far enough ahead of me that it would certainly catch me, even if I tried to run around it. I could run back to my house. But the door was locked, and unlocking it would kill any head start I had.

My only choice was to run for the street and hope Latte followed me. I would scream. The evening was early enough that the old folks on the street would still be awake and would hear me. They could look out their windows and see me running down the road, which was illuminated by the streetlights. They would call the police. I would run to Main Street if I had to. Eventually, someone would see me. I would run until someone saw me.

I tensed all my muscles, getting ready to make a break for it while trying not to let the figure see which way I was going.

I counted down in my head. Three...two... one...

"You just couldn't stay out of it, could you, Fran?" The figure spoke. The voice was familiar, male, but in my panic, I couldn't place it. I didn't run. I tried to speak, to apologize to the figure for getting involved, to beg him to leave me alone, but the fear paralyzed my vocal cords, and nothing came out.

"You just couldn't leave well enough alone." He took a step toward me now. I stepped backward, not wanting to let him get any closer than he already was. He kept coming toward me. "You had to tell everything to Mike, had to go running your mouth to him. I should have known better, but I didn't realize quite what a little tattle-tale you are."

His long legs were bringing him toward me faster than I could back away. His walk was familiar, too, as was the way he carried himself. His identity flitted around my brain but wouldn't stop long enough for me to catch it.

His arm moved to pull something out of his jacket pocket. I heard a nauseating click that I had never before heard in real life, only on TV: the sound of a gun safety clicking off. "It's too bad, you know." He stepped quickly toward me. "I always liked you."

And then I knew who it was. I recognized the laid-back tone of the voice, now tinged with aggression, and the casual swaying walk that suddenly seemed so menacing.

"Chase, please, you don't have to do this." I finally found my voice.

"Oh, I don't? You're about to bring the law down on me, and I don't have to stop you? That's where you're wrong."

"I didn't tell him it was you! I swear! I didn't even know you had anything to do with it! Why would I think that?"

"You expect me to believe that?"

"Yes! You have to! It's the truth!"

"I may be a criminal, but I'm not an idiot, Fran."

He was an arm's length away from me now. I had to do something, or I would be another case file on Mike's desk.

I did the first thing that came to mind. I kicked him. Then I hit him, just the way we learned in kickboxing class—plant your feet, twist with your hips, drive through your first two knuckles. I kicked him again.

I screamed with each blow just like our teacher had taught us.

Chase was stumbling back now, likely more surprised by the attack than he was injured by it. But if surprise was what I had going for me, I was going to use it.

I kept coming, hitting and kicking. I heard the gun fall to the ground with a thud. I heard Latte barking frantically. I kicked Chase again and landed another punch. I remembered something I should have thought of sooner and, with my next kick, planted my foot firmly in his groin. He fell to the ground, clutching himself. I kicked him again to make sure he wasn't faking it. Latte ran past me toward Matt's house then flew back my way, barking all the while. He circled me then took off toward Matt's again.

I looked at Chase on the ground and tried to figure out what to do next. If I ran, he might get away. Instead, I planted my foot on his throat with just enough force to make sure he knew it was there. He whimpered but didn't move.

Latte made another lap, and I felt in my pocket for my phone to call the police. I came up empty-handed and realized I'd put it in my purse, which I'd dropped at some point in the confrontation. I opened my mouth to scream for help, but before I could make a noise, Matt's front light came on, and his door opened.

"What the hell?" He stopped as he caught sight of me standing over Chase with Latte barking furiously in his face.

"Latte, hush!" I commanded. Latte stopped barking but kept a low growl going in Chase's direction. I looked at Matt, whose bewildered expression I could see in the light from the house. "Could you call the police? And, if you can, could you let Sammy know I'm probably not going to make it to our girls' night?"

Chapter Twenty

Three nights later—a week to the day after our first attempt—we finally managed to have our girls' night out, which had expanded a little from our first two attempts.

The group of us—me, Sammy, Matt, Dawn, the guy bartender from the Sand Bar, Mike, his wife Sandra, and Ryan—had taken over the back deck at Fiesta Mexicana. Appetizer plates were scattered across the tables, intermixed with bowls of chips, salsa, queso, and guacamole. We each had drinks planted in front of us: beers for Matt, Mike, and Ryan; tequila shots for Dawn and her bartender friend; and margaritas for Sammy, Sandra, and me.

"I'd like to propose a toast!" Dawn announced, lifting her shot glass in the air. Bartender Guy raised his glass with her, and the rest of us quickly followed. "To Sammy! To her freedom and to second chances at celebrating it."

"Um, third chance," I corrected her.

"It only counts as the second because you guys didn't invite me to the last one!" Dawn said in the exact same tone she'd used for the toast. "To Sammy!" she repeated.

"To Sammy!" we all echoed and took a drink.

Dawn nudged me. "Your turn," she said.

I looked at her in confusion, but she gave me a "hurry up" look, so I raised my glass. "Uh, to Dawn! For arranging this night out!"

"To Dawn!" everyone repeated.

Dawn looked at Matt. He thought for a minute then raised his glass again. "To Mike! For not arresting my girlfriend for beating the crap out of a guy!" We drank.

"To good times with good friends!" Sammy offered without prompting.

"To Cape Bay!" Ryan declared.

"To Fran, for catching the murderer!" Sandra said. I blushed. Mike rolled his eyes, but I saw the hint of a smile on his face as he glanced at me.

"To not having any more murders for Fran to meddle in!" Mike toasted, his slight smile breaking into a grin.

"I can drink to that," I muttered.

Dawn nudged Bartender Guy next to her when it became clear he wasn't going to realize it was his turn. "Go!" she hissed.

"To tequila!" he said, and we drank. "Excuse me," he said, standing up. "I gotta hit the head."

I watched as he left the patio then leaned over to Dawn. "Hey, what's his name?"

"You don't know?"

"You didn't introduce him."

"It's Dave."

"Ah, okay." I gestured back and forth between Dawn and Dave's empty chair. "Are you and Dave, uh, seeing each other?"

Dawn made a face. "No, Dave's gay."

"But I saw him flirting with all the girls at the bar the other night."

"You get better tips when you flirt." She smirked.

"I guess that makes sense." I leaned back in my chair.

"You get better service when you flirt, too," she said as the waiter came out with another round of drinks. "Thank you, Javier," she cooed then smiled and batted her eyelashes a couple of times.

"I brought you some empanadas." He set the plate down. "On the house."

"Aren't you the sweetest!" Dawn looked at me knowingly as he walked away. "See, I told you." She took a bite of empanada.

I shook my head and took an empanada before offering the plate to Matt.

"So, Mikey," Dawn said a few minutes later after Dave had returned from the restroom. I saw Sandra's eyes get big as she glanced at Mike. Clearly, she was just as surprised as I had been the first time I'd heard Dawn call him that. Mike narrowed his eyes a little bit in Dawn's direction but otherwise let it go. "I know Chase killed the guy in the alley, and Franny beat the snot out of Chase, but there's a lot of other things in that story I don't know. How about you fill us in?"

Mike glanced around the table then shrugged. "It's not like it won't be in the paper soon enough anyway." He inhaled deeply then blew out a breath. "So, we've known for a while—"

"Wait, who's we?" Dawn interjected.

"The Cape Bay Police Department," Mike said sternly, apparently not fond of being interrupted. I almost wanted to warn him that it would probably not be the last time Dawn jumped into the middle of his story, but I had a feeling that would come as no surprise. "So, the Cape Bay Police Department has known for a while that there were drugs coming into town—I told Fran this back before we made the arrest. Pharmaceutical stuff, mostly painkillers, but some benzos and barbiturates."

"Some whats?" Dawn asked.

Mike took a breath. I guessed he was resisting the urge to say something unkind to her. "Benzodiazepines and barbiturates." Dawn looked at him blankly. "Valium and sleeping pills."

"Oh, okay," she said. "Go on."

Mike took another deep breath. "It's been fairly steady for a while now, but there have been some spikes and drop-offs here and there. Most recently, we confiscated some during an arrest that the lab said were so long expired they were basically placebos. Sugar pills!" he added before Dawn could say anything.

"I knew that one." She smiled, and I saw Sandra stifle a giggle.

"Anyway, we knew the drugs were coming in from the outside, and, at the quantities we were seeing, they weren't just people with legal prescriptions selling off the individual pills. This had to be organized. There had to be a source—a drug manufacturer or a sales rep—or as it turned out in this case, a pharmacist. The Boston PD is still looking into how Casey managed to get the quantities of drugs that he did and move them through his pharmacy without alerting the feds to what was going on. But he was the source of the drugs, and Chase Williams was the local dealer. The kingpin, really—he sold them all down the coast and out on Cape Cod. Those rich kids apparently have quite a taste for this stuff."

"How did Chase and Casey know each other?" I asked, risking the wrath of Mike.

"Good question!" Mike said. Dawn shot me a dirty look for getting Mike's approval on my question. I gave her back my best teacher's pet smile. "It turns out," Mike continued, "that Casey used to work in the same hospital as Chase's sister Cheryl. Cheryl took Chase with her to a holiday party once before she was married, and that's when he met Casey. They've been working together for years now. Chase used his work at the salon as a front—no one would ever question him singling out a special bottle of 'shampoo' for a customer or giving them a sample of a product. He'd put the pills in a baggie and slip them into the shampoo bottle or the sample container, and the customer would pay him cash or include it in his tip. Apparently, he was really good at cutting hair, so no one thought twice about him making a lot in tips."

Around the table, the women nodded. "If I wasn't married to his arresting officer, I'd say that losing Chase as a hair stylist is a real blow to the community," Sandra said. Mike looked at her as though he thought she had lost her mind. "But I am married to him," she rushed to say, "so I understand fully how important it is that he's off the streets." Mike nodded and looked away from her. She leaned back in her chair so he couldn't see her, made a sad face, and wiped a mock tear from her eye. Sammy,

Dawn, and I all looked away so Mike didn't see us laugh.

"Anyway, I had mentioned that the worthless batch had been circulating around town. Chase realized that it was bad, and when Casey came to deliver the next batch, Chase confronted him about it and told him that he wasn't paying this time since he'd paid the last time and gotten a bad product. Casey refused, they argued, then they parted ways. The next day, Chase came looking for Casey for another attempt at 'negotiations.' This time, he brought a gun to try to be a little more persuasive. Casey still wouldn't back down, and Chase shot him. Says it was an accident, but I'm not so sure about that."

"What was with the suicide thing?" Dawn asked.

Mike didn't even seem to flinch at this interruption, now engrossed in telling his story. "Chase knew that Casey had lied to his wife about where he was going. He knew Casey had hooked up with Suzy from the Sand Bar the night before. He figured there was enough evidence along those lines to make suicide plausible, as long as no one looked too close, so he put the gun in Casey's hand and walked away. Why he thought we wouldn't do an autopsy or check for gunshot residue, I don't know. As long as he kept his drug trade going, you'd think he'd be a little better at covering up his crimes, but I guess his incompetence is just something for us to be grateful for."

"So, did you know it was him before he attacked Fran?" Matt asked.

"Not a clue. We were pursuing other leads. We might have figured it out eventually, but I can't be sure. If he hadn't attacked Fran, he might have gotten off scot-free."

"Why did he come after me?" I asked. "I never told you anything about him. I thought it was the wife."

"Apparently, he saw you talking to me after your haircut the other day. I guess he'd just offered you some pills and thought that you were ratting him out. He thought that if we came after him for that, the whole thing would come crashing down on him, so he decided to eliminate the witness."

"Even though he thought I'd already told you what happened?"

Mike shrugged. "Criminals don't always think the clearest."

"Suzy's going to be mad that her drug supply's dried up," Dawn said.

"I'm sure she'll find a way to get them," Mike said. "There's too much of a demand for stuff like that for the supply to dry up for too long. All we can do is keep it off the streets the best we can."

We all sat and let Mike's information sink in.

"So," Sammy said thoughtfully, "Fran really is kind of responsible for the case getting solved. If she hadn't gotten involved, you might never have figured out who the murderer was."

"We would have gotten it eventually," Mike said.

"But you solved it faster because of Fran."

"Civilians should leave police business up to the police." Mike cast a look in my direction.

"I can't help that I get curious!" I said. "I just saw that souvenir bag and knew there had to be something more to the case. And then Mary Ellen told me about the marzipan and—well, who buys marzipan without planning to eat it? That stuff is delicious!"

"She has good instincts. You have to give her that," Ryan said.

Mike shook his head and looked at me. "And I don't care how good your instincts are. I'm not inviting you to work on a case any time soon."

"She was helpful, though, wasn't she, Mike?" Sandra prompted.

He looked at Sandra for a second as though she'd just shared with all of us what kind of underwear he preferred. She smiled a lovely smile at him. He turned back to me. "You were helpful, even if it was by accident."

I smiled at him, accepting his indirect compliment. I knew better than to push my luck.

"I think I'm going to sign up for Fran's kickboxing class on Monday," Sandra said.

"I'll get you a gun," Mike said.

"Chase had a gun," I pointed out. "I just had a few kickboxing lessons and a lot of adrenaline."

Mike grunted.

Our conversation faded into silence.

Matt took my hand. "I'm glad you're safe," he whispered and lifted my hand to his lips.

I smiled at him and took a sip of my margarita. It was perfect. It was served on the rocks, just the way I liked it. Between that, the cool salt air blowing in off the water, and the friends surrounding me, I didn't think I could be any happier.

Recipe 1: Marzipan

Makes 12 ounces

Ingredients:
- 1 ½ cups almond flour/meal
- 1 ½ cups powdered sugar
- 2 teaspoons pure almond extract
- 1 teaspoon food-grade rose water
- 1 egg white

Pulse almond flour and sugar in a food processor until fully combined with no lumps. Add almond extract and rose water. Pulse again to combine. Add egg white, and process until a thick dough is formed. If the dough is still wet and sticky, add more sugar or ground almonds. If the dough is flimsy, it will become firmer after refrigeration.

Knead almond marzipan on a work surface. Shape into a log. Wrap in plastic wrap and refrigerate. It will keep for a month in the fridge or up to six months in the freezer.

Marzipan can be dipped in chocolate. If you're artistic, you can shape marzipan into fruits, vegetables, figurines, or anything you'd like.

Recipe 2: Classic Margarita on the Rocks

9 servings

Ingredients:

- 2 ounces tequila
- 1 ounce Cointreau
- 1 ounce fresh lime juice
- Salt for garnish

Combine tequila, Cointreau, and lime juice in a cocktail shaker with ice. Moisten the rim of a cocktail glass with lime juice or water. Hold the glass upside down and dip into salt. Strain drink into glass and serve.

Recipe 3: Frozen Straw-berry Margarita

9 servings

Ingredients:
- 3 ½ cups strawberries
- 2 ½ cups crushed ice
- ½ cup tequila
- ½ cup fresh lime juice
- ¼ cup sugar
- 3 tablespoons Cointreau
- Lime wedges (optional)

Combine strawberries, ice, tequila, lime juice, sugar, and Cointreau in a blender. Process until smooth. Pour margaritas into four large glasses. Garnish margaritas with a lime wedge, if desired.

About the Author

Harper Lin is the USA TODAY bestselling author of *The Patisserie Mysteries*, *The Emma Wild Holiday Mysteries*, *The Wonder Cats Mysteries*, and *The Cape Bay Cafe Mysteries*.

When she's not reading or writing mysteries, she loves going to yoga classes, hiking, and hanging out with her family and friends.

www.HarperLin.com

35740365R00178

Made in the USA
San Bernardino, CA
02 July 2016